ESSAYS,

SHORT STORIES AND POEMS

—BY—

MISS M. S. SNELL,

INCLUDING A

SKETCH OF THE AUTHOR'S LIFE

Friends of The Head Harbour Lightstation

PRESERVE, PROTECT AND PROMOTE

ISBN 978-1-937720-22-3

First published 1881
This edition published 2014

Produced for Friends of the Head Harbour Lightstation
by
Sea Hill Press Inc.
www.seahillpress.com
Santa Barbara, California

Printed in the United States of America

FOREWORD.

— § —

In mid-1842, an immigrant family—father, mother, son, and baby daughter—crossed the north Atlantic from England to make a home in the Maritime province of New Brunswick. The father, William Snell, would soon become the second lightkeeper of the Head Harbour Lightstation on Campobello Island. His daughter, Mary, spent her youth at the Lightstation, and, in this volume, recounts the story of her life as the lightkeeper's daughter. Today the Lightstation is a beautiful site to visit. The craggy seashore, dense pine woods, and sea mist shrouding the tower and outbuildings add an aura of mystery and romance to these historic structures. But Mary's story makes the wood and stone come alive with her voice.

Head Harbour Lightstation is perched on the outermost of a group of small rocky islets at the northeastern tip of Campobello Island, in New Brunswick, Canada. It is the oldest surviving lighthouse in New Brunswick. The setting can be deceptively peaceful on days of clear skies, bright sun, and calm winds. The glassy seas may mirror brilliant blue skies; whales and porpoises may frolic offshore; eagles, cormorants, and gulls may glide overhead. But it is often dangerously cold and windy, with storms lashing the granite outcroppings and battering the tower and outbuildings. Standing at the entrance to the Passamaquoddy Bay in the Bay of Fundy, the Lightstation endures some of the world's highest and most violent tides. Whirlpools await the unwary, high winds gust through the channel, and the waters are chilled by the icy Labrador Current. Though only a few hundred feet from the body of Campobello Island, Lightstation dwellers are isolated from their neighbors since the islet is accessible by land bridge for only a few hours surrounding low tides. Because of the rocky shoals, looming cliffs, and dearth of natural anchorage, access by boat is always limited, and impossible during stormy weather and high seas. Without the conveniences of telephone, satellite, or internet communication, the lightkeeper and his family were cut off from the rest of the world for much of the time.

Campobello Island was first settled by European immigrants in the late seventeenth century. Nearby St. Croix Island was the site of a short-lived colony established by Samuel de Champlain in 1604, and Campobello Island itself appears to have been first successfully settled in the 1680s by a few French colonists. On the Island, those colonists would have met members of the Passamaquoddy tribe, descendants of the Abanakis, who made seasonal forays onto the Island to fish in the spring and summer and to hunt in the fall and winter—returning regularly until at least the late nineteenth century. Although a few French settlers drifted to Campobello over the next several decades, the Island was ceded to the English by the 1713 Treaty of Utrecht, which gave the whole of "Nova Scotia or Acadia" and "all the dependencies of the said lands and islands in those parts" to England. The English did not rush to settle the Island. By the 1760s most of the French colonists had left and only a few English families had arrived, by way of New England, to establish a settlement there.

In September 1767, William Owen, a younger son of the hereditary line of Owens of Glansevern, Wales, and a Captain in the Royal Navy, was granted the entire "Great

Outer Island of Passamaquoddy," by his patron, Lord William Campbell, Governor-in-Chief, Captain General and Vice-Admiral of Nova Scotia. In the grant, Owen was named the "Principal Proprietary" of the Island. To honor his patron for this land grant, much larger than the entitlement for a military officer of his rank at the time, Captain Owen punningly re-named his island "Campo Bello." Grateful though he was for this compensation, Owen did nothing to exploit his grant for the next two years. In 1769, Owen solicited from his English acquaintances subscriptions to establish a company, purchase and outfit a vessel, and recruit Lancashire families, most of them indentured servants, to settle the Island. The colonists arrived in June 1770 and were soon joined by additional settlers from New England. But in 1771 Captain Owen returned to England, and by late 1772 only nine of the original 38 Lancashire settlers remained on the Island. The Island remained virtually unmanaged for the next fifteen years. Captain William Owen was succeeded as Principal Proprietary by his nephew, David Owen, in 1787, who established residence and governed the Island until his death in 1829.

Life on Campobello has long been concentrated on the seas. The soil is rocky and generally thin, underlain by granite ledges and not suitable for large-scale farming. Some livestock could forage for fodder, but trade in fish, lumber, and, later, smuggled goods, was the historic source of livelihood for Island residents. The treacherous waters of the Passamaquoddy Bay, especially at its northeastern gateway, challenge the maintenance of a lucrative trade.

Although the establishment of a lighthouse at Head Harbour had been proposed as early as July 1785 by Gillam Butler, a Boston Loyalist who purchased the northeastern portion of the Island at about that time, no lighthouse was actually constructed until shortly before David Owen's death in 1829. Just two months before he died, David Owen conveyed "to his Majesty a plot of land on the Northeast extreme of Campo Bello on which the lighthouse has been erected, being one acre of land."

Life at the Lightstation could be difficult, dangerous, and solitary. The Lightstation islet itself is barely an acre in size, much of which is covered by granite rocks and ledges. Although early lightkeepers kept some livestock, there is hardly room for a small garden, much less sufficient chickens or cows to feed a sizable family. There is no source of fresh water on the islet. Rain water was collected as runoff from the roofs of some of the buildings and held in cisterns in building cellars to provide water for the Lightstation and household use. Storms and high winds were frequent, and threatened not only the ships working their way through Head Harbour Passage but the Lightstation and its inhabitants as well. The first lightkeeper suffered the loss of his boat, firewood, barn, and cow in a March 1830 gale during which the sea broke nearly halfway up the 51 foot lighthouse tower—which itself stands on a rock nearly twelve feet above ordinary tides. While Mary Snell and her family lived at the Lightstation, another strong gale swept away the lightkeeper's boat and one of the outbuildings, with sea water breaking windows and flooding several inches of the house's first floor, while the family remained trapped on the islet.

The first keeper of the newly-constructed light was John Snell, who tended the light from at least 1830 until the mid-1840s. There is no known relationship between this John Snell and Mary Snell's family. In the early years of the Lightstation, the keeper lived in the light tower itself. Quarters would have been cramped, with much of the floor space taken up by the stairways to the lantern room and storage of supplies for the light. Built almost entirely of wood with a stone and masonry foundation, the light tower would have been ripe for destruction by fire—from the light itself or from stoves and lighting in the keeper's household. The construction of a separate keeper's house in 1840 not only gave the keeper's family much more comfortable quarters but also reduced the risk of fire in the tower.

The lightkeeper's house is an attractive dwelling, typical of working-class homes of the mid-nineteenth century. It has a parlor area, dining room, and kitchen on the first floor and three dormer bedrooms on the second floor. It would have been comfortable, but not commodious for the growing Snell family. William Snell and his wife, Elizabeth, made the Atlantic crossing with their son John, who was three or four years old at the time of the voyage, and their toddler daughter, Mary. Within a couple of years, John and Mary were joined by younger brother William, and soon after by brother George. The family lived together at the Lightstation until the death of Mary's father in 1859. He was succeeded by his son John as lightkeeper, and the family continued to live at the Lightstation until John had married and brought his wife there. By that time, the keeper's house would have become too crowded—with six adults sharing the space—and so Mary, her mother, and her two younger brothers moved to a farm her father had purchased on the main island of Campobello, within easy walking distance of the Lightstation.

Mary's brother John served as the Head Harbour lightkeeper until sometime in the 1870s. He was followed by a succession of keepers and assistant keepers until the light and foghorn were automated over 100 years later. The last lightkeeper left Campobello in 1986.

Mary's life at the Lightstation was not without incident. In addition to the storms the family weathered, Mary suffered a serious illness at age seven that deprived her of sight. Yet, in spite of her blindness, Mary lived a full life. She knit and sewed, hooked rugs, played the accordion and melodeon, walked the paths and meadows of Campobello, and enjoyed the society of her neighbors. Mary's parents appear not to have coddled her or even to have made many concessions to her limitations, as she describes playing with her pet kitten, tending her flock of chickens, fishing from the Lightstation rocks, and exploring the islet—all after her illness and the resulting blindness. Mary also taught herself to read despite her loss of sight. She describes having been given a copy of the Gospel of St. John "in embossed letters for the blind," which she then learned to trace and decipher. Most likely the embossed letters were Boston Line Type, a system developed by Samuel Gridley Howe, founder of the Perkins School for the Blind in Massachusetts. Instead of the raised dots used in the Braille system, Boston Line Type consists of angular Roman type, without capital letters, embossed on heavy paper. It was the predominant writing system for the blind at the time Mary would have been learning to read and for many years after and fits her description of an "embossed letter" system.

After living for several years at the farm on Campobello, Mary and her family moved to Chatham, Ontario, to be closer to their extended family. Relatives of Mary's father had already moved from New Brunswick to this southern Ontario community, and her mother had no relatives in North America. So Mary, her mother, and her two younger brothers, then in their late 20s, moved to Chatham, later to be joined by her brother John. Mary and her family lived in Chatham until her mother's death in 1888. Mary's brother George eventually moved to Detroit, Michigan, but Mary continued to live in the town with her brother William until her death in 1910. William remained a resident of Chatham until his death some years later. Mary, her mother, and brothers John and William are all buried in Chatham's Maple Leaf Cemetery.

Mary's story gives us an insight into life at the Lightstation that the architecture and artifacts alone cannot provide. Graced with courage and a quiet determination, bolstered by her faith and a supportive and loving family, this young woman who could so easily have descended into melancholia or self-pity made for herself a rich and fulfilling life—brimming with work, friends, and accomplishments.

Her obituary in the December 16, 1910, edition of the *Chatham Daily Planet* notes that "her death is keenly regretted by many friends," and it seems clear from her own account that this was not a mere platitude but an indication of her active involvement in the community in which she chose to live.

Many people helped in this republication of Mary's story. In particular, thanks are due the members of the Board of Trustees of the Friends of the Head Harbour Lightstation: Robert and Cindy Hooper, Leo and Deanna Baldwin, Lewis and Linda Brown, Jan Meiners, Joyce Morrell, Evelyn Bowden, and Mary Albright. Special thanks are due to Joyce Morrell who prepared the scratchboard illustrations that enhance this publication. The artistry of her work and the details of the technique itself deserve their own foreword.

In Mary's day, the Lightstation was painstakingly maintained by a full-time resident lightkeeper employed by the government. Today, the Lightstation is lovingly restored and maintained by the Friends, whose mission is to "preserve, protect and promote" the unique heritage of the Lightstation for this and future generations. We are most fortunate to have discovered Mary's story and are pleased to share it with you. We believe its republication preserves the heritage of the Lightstation and of Maritime Canada in a way no paint or concrete or steel ever could. We hope you agree.

Friends of the Head Harbour Lightstation
Campobello Island, New Brunswick
January, 2014

ESSAYS,
SHORT STORIES AND POEMS

—BY—

MISS M. S. SNELL,

INCLUDING A

SKETCH OF THE AUTHOR'S LIFE

This work may be all the more interesting owing to the fact that Miss Snell is blind, having lost her sight when about Seven years of age.

Originally published by
CHATHAM
BANNER STEAM PRINT, 153 KING STREET WEST.

1881.

PREFACE.

The stories contained in this small volume are true. Nearly all of them were related to me at different times by my mother, they being incidents that came under her notice in earlier days, while living in England, and are given just as they happened, with but little or no coloring, the real names of persons and places only being withheld.

I have striven to make this little book interesting to both old and young. If I succeed I shall be glad, and if, though beyond my expectations, anything edifying can be gleaned from its pages, I shall be doubly repaid for my trouble. With good will to all, I have carefully avoided saying aught that might in any way tend to mislead or offend others, while on the other hand I have sought to uphold and promote, as far as lies in my power, all that is good and pure, having charity for my watchword, and keeping truth on my side at all times.   M.S.S.

CONTENTS.

A SKETCH OF MY LIFE.

CHAP. I. – Reminiscence of childhood before losing
my sight 1

CHAP. II. – How I lost my sight 5

CHAP. III. – How I amused myself the first seven
or eight years after losing my sight 9

CHAP. IV. – A description of the view from the
Lighthouse with an account of a violent storm
I experienced while living there 17

CHAP. V. – My trip to Boston with other recollections
of the past 29

SKETCHES AND POEMS.

More Blessed to Give than to Receive 39

Speak Gently of the Erring 40

The Fairies—a poem 42

Joe Summers 44

Advice to a Young Friend—a poem 46

xvi   CONTENTS

A Hurricane at Night 47
An Excursion Song 50
A Dream 50
Beauty in All Seasons—a poem 52
Grandma's Story, or the Child's Faith 54
Lines to the Memory of My Cousin, Sarah H. Jarvis 56
Almost Home 57
Perseverance, or the Feeble One Protected—a poem 60
The Acorn and the Oak 62
Morning Meditations 64
Evening Meditations 66
The Ruined City—a poem 69
The Islands of the Bay of Fundy 70
Arthur to Nancy—a poem 76
The Discomfited Lover 77
The Rose—a poem 80
A Welcome to Spring—a poem 80
Memory 82
How the Passamaquoddy Indians Win Their Brides . 84
To a Friend about to Cross the Ocean—a poem 85
My Mother's Story about Her Bible 86
God Seen in All His Works—a poem 89
Fretting Without Cause 92
Shamming Insanity 95
Set Down That Glass—a poem 98
The Slave's Lament—a poem 100
My Grandfather 101
Letter 106
Contention between the Life and Death Angel 111

Luke Anson 114

Blighted Flowers—a poem 121

Sweet Content—a poem 122

The Evening Breeze 123

A Conversion in a Barber Shop 123

Learning to Dive 126

To the Memory of Little Rosa 128

Annie Bowden 129

The Song of the Indian 132

The Birds 133

Lines on the Death of a Friend 135

The Child's Prayer 137

The Scoffer Converted 139

The Blessings of the Sabbath 141

Lines on the Death of a Friend 143

My Island Home—a poem 144

The Dying Child—a poem 146

Evening Charms—a poem 147

A SKETCH OF MY LIFE.

— § —

CHAPTER I.

REMINISCENCE OF CHILDHOOD BEFORE LOSING MY SIGHT.

I was born in 1841, in a small town called Seaham Harbor, County of Durham, in the North of England. When I was about a year and a-half old my parents came to America.

Immediately on our arrival my father was appointed keeper of the Head Harbor Lighthouse. The Lighthouse is situated on the North-east point of the island of Campobello, in the Bay of Fundy, County of Charlotte, and Province of New Brunswick.

There I spent my childhood and early womanhood. How many scenes of blithe, happy, innocent childhood remain fresh in the recollection even unto the end of life! When looking back in after years, childhood appears like a rosy bower, far away in the distance, radiant and glorious in the fair light of the rising sun of life's early morning. Like all other children, I was fond of the beautiful, and a more ardent admirer of nature could scarcely be found in a child, or a more silent one. I studied the force of nature with deep interest, never making a remark or asking a question. It would seem as though I instinctively felt that I would not always enjoy the blessing of sight, and eagerly sought to satisfy my soul with long and earnest gazing on the beauty and grandeur of creation, just as one takes a last farewell look; and even now, though years have passed, yet, fair as a picture fresh from the hand of the artist, is engraven on my memory my childhood home and its surroundings. The blue sky, the green fields, and the distant hills, the long sandy shore, the high steep rocks, their rugged sides covered with seaweed, and the rippling tide ever sweeping around the point, where stood the Lighthouse, ever hurrying on its way to and from the Atlantic. All this, and more, is as plain in my mental vision as if I had but recently looked upon the scene. How often, when stormy winds disturbed the deep blue water of the broad bay, have I watched the great waves as they came rolling in and dashing against the solid rocks, flung the white spray high in the air; thus, as one wave succeeded another, they formed a line of foam which encircled the island like a snowy wreath, while the roar of the breakers was music deep and grand. At other times, on a fair summer's morning when the sea was calm, I have looked eastward where the sun, pouring its bright rays on the smooth surface of the bay, made it appear in the distance like liquid gold, while nearer the shore the clear water reflected the deep blue of the sky, forming a very pleasing and interesting sight. I was fond of flowers, and when they were in bloom I marked the beauty of each and all, but, unlike other children, I never wished to gather them, for well I knew they would wither in my hand, and I would much rather see them fresh and bright.

I especially admired the pansy with its soft velvet leaves and varied hues, always looking up so sweet and modest. I also loved to watch the wild birds hopping among the grass or flitting from tree to tree, chirping and singing their happy songs. A clear summer sunset sky never failed to attract my attention. Oft and long have I gazed on that beautiful sight, and as the gold and crimson faded in the west, and as the deeper shades of night drew on, I would watch the stars as they came out one by one until the whole sky was spangled with those tiny lamps. To those who have always enjoyed the blessing of sight these things may seem scarce worth recalling, but to me it is like telling a pleasant dream. I love to think of these happy days, but seldom speak of them. I was a sober-minded child; those who knew me said I was old-fashioned and wise beyond my years. It may have been that the great sorrow that was to sadden my life cast its shadow over my soul, making my young heart less joyous than the hearts of children generally are.

CHAPTER II.

HOW I LOST MY SIGHT.

At the early age of seven I was deprived of sight during a short illness. I first complained of a severe pain over my eyes. As I grew worse a physician was called in, but he could do nothing to give relief. After a day or two the pain left my head and, passing down the back of my neck, finally ceased, leaving me as weak and helpless as an infant. It was not discovered that I had lost my sight until one morning after I began to recover. I asked my mother why she did not light a lamp, saying it is always dark now and you never light a lamp. These words startled and surprised her, for the morning was far advanced, and the sun was shining brightly into the room where I lay. My mother, fearing the worst, came to my bedside and tried various means to attract my notice, but failed. My sight was gone.

My parents were much grieved that such an affliction had come upon their only daughter, but for a long time entertained the hope that with returning strength and the aid of a skillful physician my sight would be restored. Many physicians were consulted, but all to no purpose. Some at once pronounced the case hopeless, saying the severe pain I had suffered in my head had withered the optic nerve, and medical treatment would avail nothing, but only tend to weaken my constitution. Some tried their skill, but in vain, and my parents were obliged to give up all hopes of my sight ever being restored. When I had regained my usual health and strength I soon learned to go about my own home, both in doors and out, almost as well as if I could see. I was quite happy; for while a child I did not fully realize the loss of my sight, feeling sure that when I grew up to be a young lady I would be able to see. But it was not so. After losing my sight I was forced to depend mainly on the sense of touch and hearing, both of which soon became very acute. I could no longer see sights, but I could hear sounds. I could listen to the song of the wild birds, and feel the warm sunshine, and as I walked over the green grassy fields in summer, I could smell the odour of the wild flowers and feel their velvety leaves. But the blue sky, the silver moon, and the twinkling stars were all blotted out of my existence. Henceforth nature was to me a sealed book, the pages of which I was no longer permitted to study and, without a murmur, I submitted to the Divine will, though at times my heart was sad and my spirit longed to look out upon the fair light of day and the beautiful world. The following lines I composed after losing my sight:—

When summer spreads its beauty,
    Though all by me unseen,
I know that trees and meadows
    And fields are robed in green.
I know the beauteous flowers
    Are opening into bloom,
When I, in passing near them,
    Inhale their rich perfume.

The birds that sing so sweetly,
    I know are very near,
When their soft strains of music
    Falls on my list'ing ear.
And when the sun is sinking
    Gently down to rest,
I know there's gold and crimson
    Gleaming in the west.

I know that darkness gathers,
    Silently around,
When the day is ended,
    And the dew is found
In the moonbeams sparkling,
    Gems of nature's store,
All from me are hidden,
    Veiled for evermore.

Flowers brightly blooming,
    Wild birds soaring high,
Verdure sweetly smiling
    Evening sunset sky.
All those charms of nature
    I shall never see,
Twilight gently falling
    Brings no change to me.

True, my life is saddened,
    Yet in prayer I find,
At the throne of mercy,
    Grace to be resigned.
When life's journey closes
    I shall soar away,
From this vale of darkness,
    To the realms of day.

Chapter III.

HOW I AMUSED MYSELF THE FIRST SEVEN OR EIGHT YEARS AFTER LOSING MY SIGHT.

I being the only girl in the family, and living in a somewhat secluded spot, I was obliged to spend the greater part of my time alone, amusing myself as best I could. My first pet was a beautiful black kitten, which was one day given to me. I was delighted with the little creature, taking care to feed it several times a day, and preparing a soft warm bed for it to sleep in. I would sit for hours with it on my lap, stroking its soft fur and listening to its low purring. As time passed the little kitten grew to be a large kitten, and a very playful one, as kittens generally are. We were very fond of each other, and spent a great deal of time together, kitty and I. One morning, after it had grown to be a fine large cat, my brother John came into the house carrying it in his arms. But, oh, sorrow, the cat was dead. It had been caught in a trap set to catch minks, and my beautiful cat was dead. I took it in my arms and going out sat down on the door step and laid it carefully on my lap, crying all the while as if my heart would break. I took its paws in my hands, but they were cold. I stroked its soft coat, but it did not move or purr—pussy was indeed dead. After my first burst of grief had somewhat subsided, my father came, and gently taking the cat from my lap, carried it away. I did not ask what he did with it; it did not matter, pussy was dead. After a few days I ceased grieving for my cat. But I have not yet forgotten my first pet.

Every little girl has one or more dolls. I usually had three or four, and a room all to myself to play house-keeping in, of which I was very proud. And no mother was ever more zealous in caring for the real needs of her children than I was to the imaginary wants of my dolls. I cut and made their clothes very nicely, so every one said who seen them.

At first I experienced much inconvenience on account of not being able to thread my needle. It prevented my sitting in the room with my dolls as I liked to do when sewing for them, and for that reason I did not sew so much as I otherwise would have done. And moreover, as now, so it was in childhood, I shrunk from wearying others with my troubles and would often amuse myself in some other way rather than be constantly teasing someone to thread my needle. So at last I determined to try and thread a needle myself, which after a long trial, to my great joy, I succeeded in doing. Thus encouraged I tried again with the same success. Again and again I unthreaded and threaded the needle, and after some little practice I could thread a needle as quickly as any one, and can do so now.

This difficulty surmounted, I spent hour after hour in my play room, sewing for my dolls, feeling quite independent and as deeply interested as if my work had been of the utmost importance. Times out of number have I been asked, "How do you thread a needle?" I always reply, I cannot tell you, nor can I explain to satisfaction how I do. I put the eye of the needle to my tongue in order to get it in a right position to receive the thread. Then I put the thread to the eye and as if by magic it goes through and the needle is threaded. This is the best explanation I can give.

Another source of amusement to me in childhood was a flock of chickens I owned, five in number. At first they were very shy when I put their food down, they would not come near to eat until I had moved quite a distance from it. But I soon won their confidence and in a few days I and my chickens were on the most friendly terms; they would come and eat out of my hands without the least fear. In fact they seemed rather to like my being among them. Whenever I went out of doors they would gather round me, all talking in their way, and which talk by my interpretation, was expressions of regard for me and confidence in my good will to them. They seemed pleased when I spoke to them or stroked their feathers. If I showed partiality by taking one upon my lap the rest would give vent to their feelings of jealousy by sundry little picks at my clothes. If I at once put down the envied chicken they would avenge themselves by not allowing it to come near me again for that time at least. If I persisted in keeping it on my lap its companions, after a little while, would walk slowly away, talking to each other in confidential tones, evidently disgusted with my lack of taste in the choice of beauty and goodness even in a chicken. Sometimes, like Kitty Clyde, I would take my line and hook and go to the brink of a steep rock and catch small fish which sported near the shore when the tide was in. But instead of the clear running brook that Kitty fished in, I threw my baited hook into the broad briny waters of the bay. When fish were plenty my time was fully taken up in catching them; now and then one would wriggle off my hook just as I had got it to the surface, which was very fortunate to the fish, but to me really provoking. After losing two or three in this way my fishing would be about done, for those who get such a scare, besides getting their mouths badly hurt with the hook, immediately struck out into deep water, and the rest taking the alarm would hastily follow suit. When fish were scarce—or, perhaps, not hungry—while I waited for them to decide whether to taste my bait or not, I mingled my voice with the murmur of the tide, as I sang some song familiar in those happy days of childhood. This was not a favorite pastime with me, owing to the fact that it yielded me as much pain as pleasure. I was pleased when I felt a bite at my hook, but as soon as I had brought the fish to land I was sorry for the suffering little creature, and taking the hook from its mouth as carefully as I could, I frequently returned it to its native element feeling more satisfied with myself for so doing.

At times, when in a listless mood, if the weather was pleasant, I would go out of doors and sit down in some spot where I could listen to any sound there might be to listen to. The usual sounds were the screaming of the sea gulls as they darted hither and thither, skimming the water in quest of food; the splashing of the wheels of a passing steamboat; the voices of the fishermen talking as they passed and repassed in their fishing boats, with now and then the spouting of a whale, for these great fish frequently make their appearance in the bay, often swimming along within a few yards of the shore. Sometimes the only sound to be heard was the lowing of the cattle, the bleating of sheep, or the barking of dogs on the neighbouring island. That which pleased and interested me most was the singing of the sailors while getting their vessels underway preparatory to leaving the harbor, to the entrance of which the Lighthouse is a faithful guide to the mariner by night in all seasons of the year. When a dozen or more sailors unite in singing, as they usually do when weighing anchor, their concert is well worth hearing. As their voices come floating over the water, borne on the wings of a summer breeze, there is a softness and richness imparted to the strains which cannot fail to attract attention. And often have I listened with delight to those hardy sons of Neptune while they sang some one of their favorite songs—composed, for aught I know, by Neptune himself. These, I have mentioned, were my chief amusements when alone; but, besides these, there were many other ways in which my young heart was gladdened, and many comforts I heartily enjoyed. Occasionally I would spend the day with some little girls of my acquaintance, and now and then they would visit me. Though deprived of sight I still retained my fondness for flowers, and in summer always had some growing near the door. When they were in bloom I was quite happy, trying to cheat myself into the belief that I could see them. I loved to go to Church and Sabbath School, and did so whenever I could, though it was a walk of nearly three miles. I was fond of learning by rote hymns and passages of Scripture, which I did with but little trouble, being blessed with a good memory. It gave me much pleasure to have some one read aloud to me, or join with me in singing. Possessing quite a good voice of my own and being very fond of music I was always pleased to learn a new tune. Thus passed my childhood unclouded by care or sorrow.

How oft back to childhood
   My memory strays,
To the morning of life,
   Those bright happy days.
Those moments all freighted
   With innocent glee,
Unmingled with care,
   And from sorrow were free,

With heart full of gladness,
   I played mid the flowers,
And sang with the birds
   Through the warm summer hours;
No thought for the morrow,
   As joyous as they,
O childhood, sweet childhood,
   How short is thy stay.

To wish to recall thee,
   Were foolish and vain,
Yet fresh in my memory
   Will ever remain,
Those scenes of my earlier,
   Happier years;
Like a beautiful picture
   To me it appears.

But childhood must pass
  With its visions so fair,
And youth with its dreams,
  And its castles in air,
Time hurries us onward
  O'er life's busy way,
To the unknown beyond,
  To eternity's day.

When clouds gather darkly
  Above and around,
When my spirit is sad,
  And trials abound,
When feeble and faint
  Is the glimmer of light
That shines on my pathway
  To guide me aright,

A voice seems to whisper,
  And tenderly say,
Fear not, I'll not leave thee
  Alone on the way;
I will lead thee to joys
  That are fadeless and pure,
Where all that is lovely
  Shall ever endure.

CHAPTER IV.

A DESCRIPTION OF THE VIEW FROM THE LIGHTHOUSE, WITH AN ACCOUNT OF A VIOLENT STORM I EXPERIENCED WHILE LIVING THERE.

The spot where Head Harbor Lighthouse stands is a small island of itself, containing not more than a half acre of land separated from the main island by a long bar, which, when the tide is out, is wide enough for a little army to cross dry shod, but when the tide is in it is covered with water to the depth of six or eight feet. The Lighthouse is a wooden building, sixty feet high, with dwelling house attached. A few yards from the door of the cottage is a large flat rock about fifteen feet in length by seven or eight at the broadest part, oval in shape and somewhat elevated. From this rock a fine view is presented to the eye. As you face the east, on your right, and within a stone's throw is Head Harbor, bounded on the opposite side by a pretty island; on the left is the entrance of the Passamaquoddy River; to the north and about three miles distant is the main land, stretching away to the eastward, its harbors, coves, and headlands appearing between numerous islands that fringe its shore. In a southeasterly direction, as far as the eye can see, there is nothing to be seen but sky and water, that being the entrance of the bay where it meets and mingles with the Atlantic Ocean—the whole forming a beautiful prospect, especially on a summer evening when the bay is thickly dotted with boats and vessels of all sizes making their way into the river or harbor. The rock already described is by no means the only one there, for there is a superabundance of them, both large and small; in fact the little island is completely surrounded with huge ledges and boulders of monstrous sizes, which do good service as breakwaters in the stormy weather of winter. I will here give an account of one storm I well remember, a gale of unusual violence, almost amounting to a hurricane. On awaking one morning in winter I heard the wind blowing heavily from the east, but being accustomed to those things I was not in the least alarmed. I arose with the rest of the family, and while breakfast was being prepared, my father remarked that if the wind increased with the rising of the tide, as it generally did, that the storm would be a fearful one. The tide in that vicinity rises and falls to the height of twenty-four feet within the limits of twelve hours—being six hours rising and six hours falling. It was now near seven o'clock, and the tide had began to rise. But there was no immediate danger, and my father engaged in family prayers, as was his custom, after which we sat down to breakfast, the storm still raging wildly. About eight o'clock my father had some thoughts of taking his family on to the main island, but hoping the tide would abate at half tide, as it sometimes did, and not wishing to take us out in the drenching rain, perhaps for nothing, he delayed doing so until it was too late; the water was over the bar, and we were obliged to remain, come what would. The storm steadily increased but did no damage until eleven o'clock; then it began its work of destruction. The Lighthouse boat was the first thing to be swept away and dashed to pieces by the waves; a small wharf soon followed, and so one thing after another went until almost everything moveable was washed away. About fifteen minutes before twelve an outbuilding used for general purposes was lifted from its foundation and thrown down on to the beach, where it remained without further injury. The storm was now at its height. If we passed the next thirty minutes in safety the danger would be over. Higher, higher came the tide; the wind seemed to have gathered all its strength for one tremendous sweep ere it finally ceased, each succeeding wave leaping nearer and nearer until they dashed fiercely against the house, breaking in the windows and flooding the lower floor with salt water to the depth of several inches. Thus, for one half hour, we waited in terrible suspense, expecting every moment the house would be swept from its foundation. My father gathered his family around him, and there, amid the roaring of the tempest, he, in fervent prayer, besought God, in whom he trusted, even that God who rules the storm, to protect us from the threatening danger.

In a few minutes more the tide had turned, the wind and waves had begun to subside, and we again

breathed free. As soon as they could cross the bar some of the neighbors came to see how we had fared. Those who were living in sight of the Lighthouse watched it anxiously all through the storm. They said the waves ran so high at times the Lighthouse could not be seen at all, and more than once it was thought to be gone. But it stood firm and uninjured; the dwelling house sustained no further damage after the windows had been broken in. Before night the storm had entirely passed away, the sun went down in a clear sky, and not a breath of wind or a ripple of the water disturbed the stillness of the evening. It may readily be supposed that I was not so brave in stormy weather after that as I had been before, though I did not experience another such a storm while living at the Lighthouse.

Being now about sixteen years of age, and no longer a child, I put away childish things. I was no longer content with merely amusing myself, but always wished to be employed in doing something useful. I began by learning to knit, but did not get along very well for quite a while. I was constantly dropping stitches or knitting two instead of only one, or putting the yarn twice over the needle when once was enough. After working in this troublesome way for an hour or so I grew discouraged, and would put away my knitting perhaps for a week or two, but being naturally active and persevering I was not apt to give up entirely if in any way I could accomplish whatever I might undertake. So I tried knitting again and again, and little by little improved until I could do plain knitting quite well, and in course of time I could knit stockings, socks and mittens as well as any one, shaping them all myself. I learned to do plain sewing with less difficulty than I experienced in learning to knit, though I pricked my finger with the needle a good deal at first, but after some practice I could sew very well. I began and finished a patchwork quilt, cutting the squares and sewing them all myself. When at this work I was obliged to sit near some one who could tell me the light pieces from the dark, and also the right side of the calico. I was a long time about it, but my quilt was done at last, and that was the only patchwork quilt I ever made. I also made quite a number of door mats and hearth rugs in those days. The first ones I braided. Then I knit two or three. After that I learned to make them with a hook. Some of my hooked mats were said to be quite pretty. I know they are very serviceable, for some of them are in wear yet.

I sometimes tried my hand at fancy work but did not do much at it. I made one wool card basket, one bead collar, and a bead necklace. I also made several pincushions, a few netted tidies, and some shell picture frames. That was about all I did in the way of fancy work. One day my father gave me an accordeon. I was much pleased with the instrument, and being very fond of music I immediately began learning to play, but having to be my own instructor I did not progress very rapidly. However, after a few months' practice I could play quite nicely, and many an hour did I spend singing and playing—as happy as a queen. Happy, because in my secluded home I was unaccustomed to the ways of the world, untainted with its vain aspirations and unacquainted with its follies and fleeting pleasures.

An artist might have painted my portrait and called me innocence, for though a woman in years, I was as unsuspecting and artless as a child. So ignorant was I of the sinfulness of human nature that never for a moment did I entertain the thought that one person would willfully wrong another. In form and features I was not homely; that could not be truthfully said of me. Neither was I beautiful; no one ever said I was; but more than once I was complimented on being pretty. Upon one occasion when in company with a young gentleman, an officer in the American navy, he asked me if I remembered my looks when I used to see my face in the looking-glass. I answered, yes. "Well," said he, "you do not know how you look now, so I must tell you you are quite pretty." This was the first time I had been told the fact by a young gentleman, and I was so embarrassed that instead of thanking him for the compliment, I blushed like a rose and said nothing. I presume he thought me the very essence of shyness and stupidity. I was extremely bashful, never speaking when in company except when spoken to, and then the shorter I could make my answer the better I was pleased. This often annoyed my parents for it made me appear dull and unsociable. Up to this time my days had passed in tranquility; though the loss of sight saddened my life, yet, being of a happy turn of mind, my young spirit was not entirely crushed. As yet not a wave of trouble had rippled the smooth surface of the river of time down which my light barque glided pleasantly.

But clouds must rise and storms of sorrow fall to

remind us that this is not our abiding place. Few tread the path from the cradle to the grave without experiencing more or less of the disappointments and trials that fall to the lot of mankind. The first grief that pierced my heart was the death of my father—but in this bereavement I mourned not as one without hope, fully assured that my loss was his infinite gain. My father was a sincere Christian, never shrinking from his duty as such, never weary in well-doing, always serving the Lord and rejoicing in His loving kindness. While living he was a man beloved and respected by all who knew him, and after death was followed to his last resting place by a large company of mourners. After a short illness he was called to lay down his cross and enter into his eternal rest. His end was peace. Without a struggle he breathed his last, without a sigh he fell asleep in Jesus. "Blessed are the dead who die in the Lord, yea, henceforth and forever."

Dear Father, thou art gone to rest,
    Life's troubled scenes are o'er,
Now safe at home among the blest,
No more by sin and doubt oppressed,
    Thy joys are rich and pure.

Dear Father, oh, I miss thee now,
    Life's happiest hours are sad,
I miss thee when in prayer we bow,
I miss thy soft kiss on my brow,
    In tenderness bestowed.

Dear Father, oh, I miss thy words
    Of kind instruction given,
To cheer me on life's weary road,
And in my heart to shed abroad
    Sweet thoughts of home and heaven.

Dear Father, I remember well
    Thy precepts and thy love,
Deep in my heart, O may they dwell,
Till from this world I soar to swell
    Thy song in heaven above.

Dear Father in the Heavenly choir
    Thy voice me thinks I hear,
And music from thy golden lyre
Doth with sweet hope my heart inspire
    To meet thee, Father dear.

Chapter V.

MY TRIP TO BOSTON WITH OTHER
RECOLLECTIONS PASSED.

As I had an ear for music and a voice for singing, it was thought by those interested that if I had a melodeon I might learn myself to play on it. So my brothers bought one and gave it to me. My friends were not disappointed, for I soon learned to play quite well considering the disadvantage of my position. I was elated with my success, and delighted to have a musical instrument of my own to practice on. Though I am only an ordinary performer, yet it has been a great source of amusement to me. I have my melodeon now, apparently as good as ever, and would not part with it for twice its value. I do not take so lively an interest in playing now as I did the first few years, still I am passionately fond of music and often spend an hour or so very pleasantly playing and singing. As I have no embossed music books I have to depend on others to read music to me, but I am not long in learning to play a tune, sometimes only a few minutes. It was about two years after I got my melodeon when my heart was again gladdened by receiving a copy of the Gospel of

St. John, in embossed letters for the blind—in two parts, kindly presented to me by R.W. Crookshank, Esq., of the City of St. John, New Brunswick.

I took one of the two books in my hand, opened it, ran my fingers over the page and soberly thought if these strokes are intended for letters how are they to be understood, for really at first they seemed to me like a confused mass of marks that might mean nothing. However, I had not the least doubt but that I should soon understand and learn to read them, and with newly awakened interest and much pleasure I turned to the first page where I found the Alphabet, and also instructions for the pupil. With my fingers I slowly traced every line of each letter, carefully noting the shape and position of them all, delighted with the prospect of learning to read so much for myself, which I was not long in doing. Before a week had passed I could read almost as well as I can now. My books are not much the worse for wear, the leaves being of very strong paper, and I take great care of them, prizing them highly for two reasons:—First, because they are a portion of the word of God; and second, for the sake of the giver, whose sympathy for and good will towards me prompted him to this act of kindness, which I shall always remember with gratitude and thanks to Mr. Crookshank.

Four years after my father's death my eldest brother married, and my mother and I, with my two younger brothers, left the Lighthouse and went to live on a small farm which my father had purchased two years previous to his death. The farm was a neck of land about a mile in length, the same from which was detached the small island where the Lighthouse stood, there being no houses between the Lighthouse and the one we lived in. This was a pleasant change to me. I could now enjoy the society of neighbors, several families living close by. Our house was situated on the top of a hill gradually sloping down to the shore on either side. On the south was Head Harbor, and on the north the Passamaquoddy River.

For many years the shore on the river side has been occupied by Indians as a camping ground. During the summer seasons the men go out in their canoes porpoise hunting, and the women sit in their camps making baskets. They are quiet and civil, never giving any trouble. They dress well, and some of them have a good English education. The men are sociable and friendly, but the women are generally shy.

Strangers, who at different times come to Head Harbor in vessels from the State of Massachusetts, and distant parts of Maine, spoke to me of Professor Williams, of the City of Boston, the well-known oculist, telling me of many cases of blindness they had known cured by him, and advising me to lose no time in going to consult him. At first I did not think much about it, knowing that so many physicians had pronounced my case hopeless, and also remembering that my father, several years previous to his death, had written to Dr. Williams, describing my case and asking his advice, and in reply had received no encouragement. Knowing this, I feared the journey would be a useless one. But being urged from time to time, I began to have a desire to go to Boston; thinking, if Dr. Williams could examine my eyes, the case might prove not so hopeless as he had judged it to be by a written description, and perhaps my sight might be restored. As days and weeks passed I grew more and more anxious to go, and at last, in company with my eldest brother, I left home for Boston on the steamer *New England*; the Captain kindly giving me a free passage to that city and back. It was a voyage of nearly four hundred miles. The weather was pleasant, with a moderate breeze. But I am never sea-sick, and had my mind not been so agitated with hopes and fears as to what the result of my interview with Dr. Williams would be, I would have enjoyed the trip; as it was the hours passed slowly, and I spent a sleepless night. I was glad when morning came; it was not so lonely when the people were talking and moving about. At six o'clock in the evening we landed in Boston. A short drive in a cab brought us to the hotel, and sick with excitement, and weary with travelling, I retired to rest. As soon as my head was on the pillow I fell into a sound sleep. I will here relate what I have never before mentioned. About midnight I was suddenly awakened, the room was filled with a soft and heavenly light; my troubled spirit was at rest; my inmost soul was flooded with exquisite bliss and perfect peace pervaded my whole being. I was not alone; my father was with me, in spirit, strengthening me for the coming trial in tender and loving tones. I heard his dear, familiar voice saying unto me, "fear not for I will be with you."

And then another voice firmly but gently said, "Be still and hear what I the Lord thy God will say unto thee." Ages might have passed unheeded could I have remained wrapt in such holy ecstasy. But as the last sentence was finished, suddenly as I had been awakened, I fell asleep, sleeping soundly until morning.

Doubtless the general opinion of those who read this will be that it was a dream. Perhaps it was. If so, it was no ordinary dream, for I was perfectly conscious. As I have before said, I was suddenly awakened and as suddenly fell asleep. The dream, if such it was, occupied not more than two minutes. The rest of the night I slept soundly, not having slept before for about forty hours. That day at twelve o'clock I met Dr. Williams in his office. After examining my eyes he and my brother went into the next room. I could hear them talking but could not hear what was said. They soon returned and I asked the Doctor if he thought anything could be done to restore my sight. He replied, he was afraid not. This was sufficient to convince me that he could give no hope, but was too considerate to say so. He accompanied us to the door, kindly shook hands with me, and expressed his sympathy by saying he was sorry he could give me no encouragement. I thanked him, and said it could not be helped.

On reaching the hotel I went immediately to my room. Once there, I could no longer restrain my grief, but burst into a passionate fit of weeping, and for a time the bitterness of my disappointment was so overpowering that I lost all self-control. Again and again I wished that I might die there and then. My brain seemed on fire, and my heart was near breaking. It was the crushing of a last hope, and in the darkness of despair I thought of death as a sweet release. I thought of the grave as a place of calm repose. My tears fell like rain; it was well they did, for in my excessive grief had that fountain been sealed, reason must have deserted her throne, or a severe fit of illness been the result of so fearful a trial. The paroxysm lasted over an hour and when at length it began to subside I thought of the occurrence of the previous night, and as I recalled the sweet vision, I grew more calm, strength of mind gradually returned, and I regained self-possession. After a short time I was to outward appearance quite composed, nor did any fresh outburst of sorrow accrue until the evening when, as I sat alone in one of the great parlors of the hotel, I again wept, not passionately now, but quietly, my tears falling fast but silently. The storm had passed, but my saddened spirit could not restrain its fretting, even as the sea continues its moaning after the tempest has subsided, seeming to grieve that it had been so ruthlessly disturbed. The next morning at eight o'clock, I was again on board the steamer *New England*, and soon on my way home, where, in due time, I arrived safely. It was not until then that I learned the decided opinion of Doctor Williams. It was this. He said the optic nerve was so completely withered that it was beyond human skill to restore it. Weeks and months passed before I regained my usual spirits; in fact I do not know as I have altogether done so yet, for before visiting Professor Williams I had heard the opinion of none but ordinary physicians, and secretly cherished a faint hope that the skill and experience of a professed oculist, should I ever have the opportunity of consulting one, might effect a cure, where ordinary physicians knew no remedy in the case. But that hope was entirely swept away after my trip to Boston.

My home on the farm at Head Harbor was a pleasant one. The six years I spent there I shall always remember with pleasure. It was especially refreshing on a warm summer's afternoon, accompanied by some one of my friends, to go down on the shore and sit in the cool shade of the high steep rocks, where I could hear the salt water washing gently up over the smooth pebbles with a soft rippling sound, and listen to the wild birds singing in trees growing along the edge of the bank far above my head. I also much enjoyed a walk in the evening. The road on either side was skirted with spruce and fir trees, and, as the light breeze played among the branches, and wild flowers ladened the air with their fragrance, I loved to linger by the way, and at such times was apt to grow pensive. Nor was winter entirely without its pleasure to me, for often on a pleasant evening I was agreeably surprised by a party of eight or ten, or perhaps a dozen of my young friends, who would come to see me from the village, which was about a mile and a half distant.

After the usual greetings were exchanged and some time spent in general conversation, those who could sing did so, while I played on the melodeon. Thus pleasantly passed many a winter evening in my home at Head Harbor. We were a lone family, having no kindred near, but many kind friends. All my mother's relatives are living in England, and all my father's people who are in America, except one brother and his son, are living in Chatham, Ontario. So it came to pass, after some persuasion, my mother sold her property at Campobello and we also came west, arriving in Chatham on the Nineteenth of October, 1871, where I met quite a number of relatives, uncles, aunts and cousins, from whom I had been separated for over sixteen years, they having lived in New Brunswick before coming to Ontario.

I am still residing in Chatham. My general health is good, a blessing I have always enjoyed, for which I am truly thankful. I can go about my own home as well as any one, and do nearly all the work of the house. My mother is getting advanced in years and is of a delicate constitution, so that she can do but little and very light work.

It is now thirty years since I lost my sight. Those who have always enjoyed the blessing of sight cannot know the many trials that beset the daily path of one who is deprived of that blessing, or the sense of weariness by which they are continually oppressed. But I must not murmur. "The Lord gave and the Lord taketh away, blessed be the name of the Lord."

It is the will of our Heavenly Father that some of His children should be chastened by affliction in order to prepare them to dwell in that land beyond the river.

There's a home for the weary, a beautiful home,
    A mansion so bright and so fair,
Where forever they dwell 'neath its sheltering dome,
    Free from sorrow, from toil and from care.

A beautiful home in the city of gold,
    Prepared by our Father above,
Where the King in His glory they ever behold,
    And rejoice in His pardoning love.

A beautiful home where the weary forgets
    All the trials of life's dreary way,
Where turmoil and strife never vexes or frets,
    Where nothing can fade or decay.

A beautiful home where no storms ever rise,
    Nor the winds of adversity blow,
Not even a cloud ever darkens the sky,
    There's no winter with frost and with snow.

A beautiful home where the weary may dwell,
    Secure from all dread and alarm,
Where the songs of the ransomed exalting swell,
    And each in their hands bear a palm.

A beautiful home, an eternal abode,
    A life everlasting and pure,
Where youth is renewed and its freshness restored,
    And shall ever and ever endure.

Sketches and Poems.

MORE BLESSED TO GIVE THAN TO RECEIVE.

One afternoon in summer I was sitting by an open window, which was shaded by a grape vine, a gentle breeze playing lightly with the leaves and fanning my cheeks with its cool breath. The day was pleasant, but I felt weary, and my heart somewhat sad. I was suddenly aroused from my gloomy thoughts by a rap at the door. I got up and went to see who was there. It was a poor man who said he had travelled round looking for work until his money was gone. Would I please give him something to eat. Now when a fellow creature asks me for something to eat, I cannot find it in my heart to refuse, so I brought him some food and gave him a drink of cold water. As he took it he said, "I am much obliged to you, indeed I am. Thank you, lady."

The tone of gratitude in which those words were spoken assured me they came from a thankful heart, and that little deed of kindness was rewarded ten fold. As the poor man went from the house, the thought that

I had afforded relief to one who was in need was like the sun shining through an opening in the clouds shedding a bright ray on my path, dispelling my sad thoughts at least for a time. The grateful acknowledgment of that simple act was like an angel visit to my soul, and my heart was lighter the rest of the day. Truly it is more blessed to give than to receive.

SPEAK GENTLY OF THE ERRING.

There is a beautiful poem entitled "Speak Gently to the Erring." The idea suggests itself strongly to my mind that we should not only speak gently to the erring, but also speak gently of them. A great many people, and I am sorry to say more especially the female portion of a community, when they meet, freely indulge in scandalizing any one of their neighbors who happens to be spoken of; the character of the unconscious offender is thoroughly examined, faults carefully selected and eagerly discussed. All the bad qualities are magnified and largely commented on, while the good traits, if perchance there is any in the opinion of those engaged in the discussion, are entirely forgotten or overlooked.

Ah, me, who is there among us without faults? Alas! not one. Some try to excuse themselves by saying we do not mean any harm; we know it is so, and we must talk to free our minds. This is a poor excuse. It is not only foolishly and wickedly wasting time which might and ought to be usefully employed, but it is in direct opposition to the rules of Christianity. If we cannot say any good of our neighbor, let us say nothing. It can do no good for you and I to spend an hour or two every day in privately talking over and exaggerating the errors of others. It is not one atom of benefit to the erring one, and has a strong tendency to disturb our own peace of mind, and produce and foster in our hearts the ill feelings of envy, jealousy, hatred and deceit, making us a great deal worse than those whose faults and shortcomings we have been enumerating. "Judge not that ye be not judged, for with what judgment you judge ye shall be judged again. Love thy neighbor as thyself." Whenever you are tempted to free your mind by slandering your neighbor pause and think before you speak. Consider the folly of so doing. At such a time it is wise to be silent. Remember it is a waste of words and gratifying of an evil propensity. Against those things close the door of thy heart and bar it with charity.

> Forget not thou hast often sinned,
> And sinful yet may be,
> Deal kindly with the erring one,
> As God has dealt with thee.

Rely not upon thine own strength to resist the temptation, for if you do you will surely fail, and in some unguarded hour the tempter will lead you far out of the narrow path. Look to Him who says, "My strength is sufficient for you," and when you are sorely tempted, enter into thy closet, and when thou hast shut the door pray to thy Father, who seeth in secret, and if you pray fervently and earnestly for strength and grace it will be given you, and you will come forth at peace with God and man, and in a true Christian spirit, and with tender feelings in your heart, you will be able to speak gently of the erring.

THE FAIRIES.

I.

I many times have thought about
  That tiny little race,
Heard of by all, but none as yet
  Have ever found a trace
Of what we would suppose to be
  A fairy palace ground.
I guess they never yet have built
  A castle in our land.

II.

I heard of caves all lined with pearls,
  And shells of beauty rare,
Down by the sea in distant lands,
  The fairies may dwell there.
At all events, I think they stop
  Within their homes all day,
And wander forth in moonlight hours,
  To sing and dance and play.

III.

And run about and try to catch
  The moon's bright silver beams,
Or launch some tiny shells for boats,
  And float upon the streams.
I always think they love to roam
  Best where the flowers bloom.
The lilies and the roses are,
  Their favorites, I presume.

IV.

Their laugh is music low and sweet,
  They speak in whispers too,
They tread so light they never leave
  A track upon the dew.
If any of them wish to rest
  Awhile, I do suppose
They go and lay them gently down
  Within a half blown rose.

V.

A fairy in a rose asleep,
  Oh! what a pretty sight,
Rocked gently by the passing breeze,
  Mid dewdrops shining bright.
Methinks 'tis fire-flies they train
  For steeds, and fly away
As light as nothing, free as air,
  Such tiny nymphs are they.

VI.

I think their clothes are made of leaves
  Of flowers bright and gay,
Their corsages are always green,
  I've heard the poets say.
Some make their skirts of purple leaves,
  Some are of crimson hue,
Some of the lily pure and white,
  And some of pretty blue.

VII.

They must be pretty little things,
  Dressed in such pretty clothes,
And live a pretty little life,
  But where, that no one knows.
If fairies really do exist,
  I would not wish to be
An elfin with an aimless life,
  'Twould never do for me.

JOE SUMMERS.

He was a very bashful young man, was Joe Summers, very bashful. Whenever a girl looked at or spoke to him, he would blush to the tips of his ears, but Joe took good care that did not happen very often, for he would frequently go a long way out of his road in order to keep at a distance from the dear creatures, and so avoid being under the painful necessity of encountering their bewitching glances, and returning their salutations. As for kissing a girl, why Joe never did such a thing in his life, the very thought of such an act made his brain whirl, and his heart beat wildly. Not that Joe did not like the girls, for indeed he really did like them, and when safe in the retreat of his own room he would sit by the window for hours, watching and admiring the fair damsels passing and repassing, dressed in their gay colors, looking, as he thought, like so many butterflies, and thinking how delightful it would be if he only had the courage to go among them and catch one for himself; but he had not.

One afternoon, two young ladies came to the house to take tea and spend the evening; the evening passed; it was time for the girls to be going; the night was dark, and Joe's mother in a low tone told him he must see the girls home, adding they would think him rude if he did not. As he was the only young man in the house Joe's heart beat high, but he saw there was no help in this case. Now, all the girls in the neighborhood knew Joe's failing, and those two being young and somewhat mischievous, quickly made up their minds to have a little sport at his expense. As soon as they were out on the street each of the girls seized an arm, and purposely leaning so heavy as to almost drag the poor fellow to the ground. Joe would have given all he was worth if he could have escaped, but by a superhuman effort he bore up, and they went on their way, the girls chatting gaily all the while regardless of his embarrassment and quite bewildering him.

Near the home of the girls there was a small brook. Two logs laid across served as a bridge. The trio crossed in safety, but when about to step from the logs one of the girls, partly by accident and partly from a desire to tease Joe, slipped and fell dragging him and the other girl with her. Both of the girls repressing the merriment that was nearly choking them, held on to his arms calling on him to help them up, at the same time accusing him of inattention and awkwardness. Poor Joe nearly dead with shame and confusion, after a desperate struggle, freed himself from his tormenters, and leaving them to complete their journey by themselves, ran back home as fast as he could, mentally vowing never again to be the escort of two girls at a time.

ADVICE TO A YOUNG FRIEND.

Dear friend, fair youth and health are thine,
    Improve each passing day;
Let truth around thy footsteps shine,
    Let virtue guard thy way.

Let wisdom lead thee by the hand,
    With knowledge store thy heart;
Obey thy Maker's great command,
    From every sin depart.

Shun those who strive to turn thy feet
    From wisdom's pleasant way;
And when temptations dark you meet,
    For conquering courage pray.

To youth the path of life appears
    To lead through flowery vales;
But oft those flowers are bathed in tears
    When storms of life assails.

Then go not forth in thine own might
    To tread the path of life;
Gird on the Christian's armor bright
    To shield thee in the strife.

Oh! watch and pray, for many a snare
    The temper's hand will set;
O'ercome it all by faith and prayer,
    All earthly charms forget.

Look upward to thy starry crown,
    Press forward to the prize;
Soon thou will lay thy armor down,
    And rest beyond the skies.

Then bravely fight and nobly win,
    The victor's crown and palm;
Then free from pain and toil and sin,
    Rest safe from death's alarm.

A HURRICANE AT NIGHT.

A DESCRIPTION OF A HURRICANE THAT SWEPT
OVER THE BAY OF FUNDY AND VICINITY
ON THE 4TH OF OCTOBER,
1869, LASTING ABOUT
AN HOUR.

The night winds swept in wild and fitful gusts, moaning among the forest trees, tossing and twirling their huge branches in sullen delight, as if it sought to calm its fury by rudely stripping them of their beautiful foliage.

Out on the deep blue sea the tempest lashed the water into angry billows, seething and foaming they chase each other like fierce demons, until at last they dash madly against the solid rocks or rush wildly up the pebbling shore. The dark clouds lowered low in the heavens; they drew darker and darker, and spreading more and more. Soon every twinkling star was shut out, and the soft silver light of the fair moon was hidden, veiled as it were by a thick black curtain. The pensive song of the night bird was hushed, and the little cricket ceased its chirruping, rain began to fall, at first the drops were few and far between, but ere long they came down thicker and faster, then rain fell in torrents. The gale increased to a hurricane, and now it seemed as if everything was being swept off the earth; large trees were torn up by the roots, many were snapped like dried straws and hurled yards from where they had been standing, noble pines bowed their lofty heads and fell prostrate to the ground, houses trembled as though about to be lifted from their foundation, cheeks grew pale and the hearts of the people were filled with fear. Out on the sea vessels large and small were tossed upon the waves like feathers and crushed like egg shells, many were thrown upon the rocks, others were stranded upon the beaches. The breakers roared like hungry wolves eager to devour their prey, and many a brave sailor found a watery grave with scarce a moment's warning. Many a prayer for mercy went up to heaven that night from lips that perchance had never prayed before. At length the hand of the Storm King was stayed, the awful roar of wind and wave was hushed, and anon a soft breeze floated over land and sea, the dark clouds rolled away and one by one the stars shone out, the fair moon looked calmly down and nature was again at peace. When morning dawned the sun rose bright and clear, showing ruin and desolation on every hand. The destruction of property was immense, but that was not the worst; many a loved one who were in the prime of vigor of life the previous night, had since passed away from earth forever, and were now sleeping beneath the briny waters. Time and means have restored the lost property, but God alone could heal the bleeding hearts of the widow and fatherless.

AN EXCURSION SONG.

The summer breeze is sighing on the waters now,
Our flag is gaily flying, there's gladness on each brow,
Our little bark will safely bear us o'er the wave,
We'll glide secure and swiftly with hearts both free
    and brave.

The shore is fast receding, fading from our view,
Before the breeze we're speeding, o'er waters deep
    and blue,
Our song of heartfelt gladness echoes far and wide,
We'll drive away all sadness while on the rolling tide.

A DREAM.

I passed through the low gateway, and stood in a broad and beautiful enclosure. The sod under my feet was softer and richer than the most costly green velvet. The sky was blue and cloudless, the air soft and mild and laden with a sweet odor, wafted hither by a gentle breeze. There was no need of the sun to give light, neither the moon, for a holy, heavenly light illumined the place. On the opposite side of the enclosure there was a high and shining wall, and just before me there was a great white gate, lofty and grand. The gate was ajar, and near it stood the stately warden. As I gazed on the wondrous beauties of the place, I heard sounds of music from within the shining wall, music soft and sweet, deep and melodious, such as mortal ear never listened to, stirring my inmost soul with its rich cadence. Many past in at the low gateway before and after me, forms that seemed made of light, clad in snowy garments, all going up to the great white gates, each carrying in their hands a small square piece of parchment, which they gave to the warden before passing through the shining portal. I also drew near and looked wistfully up at the pearly gate, then timidly at the warden; he fixed his mild starry eyes on me and said in a tone of pitying love and gentle reproof, "Why camest thou hither unprepared and unbidden by the King?" I bent forward in silence, for I felt that unprepared as I was and unbidden, I had no right in that holy place. The angel's hand was laid upon my bowed head and he continued, "Thou art weary of earth, thou would fain lay down thy cross and enter into thy rest, but thy race is not yet run, thy earthly mission is not yet fulfilled, return to the world and when thou art weary seek not to lay down thy cross, but pray for grace and strength from on high to sustain thee. So shalt thou hold out to the end of thy pilgrimage, and when thou hast accomplished all that the King would have thee to do, He will send a white winged messenger to summon thee and give thee thy passport and thy robe of spotless white. Then weary one come, and I will gladly admit thee into thy eternal rest." I turned slowly and sorrowfully away, and retracing my steps, passed out at the low gateway, and was again in the world. But the star of hope smiles on me, though distanced far, while the wings of faith bear me safely over every trial, and when my weary spirit essays to unfold her pinions and soar away to seek the rest she so ardently desires, I remember the words of the angel with the assurance that if I prove faithful to my mission, in the service of my King, when He summons me hence, I shall receive my white robe and

with my passport in my hand, I will again pass in at
the low gateway; then with a smile of recognition and
welcome the stately warden will admit me through
the shining portal into the celestial city, where forever
I shall dwell in the presence of the King, no more to
be weary.

BEAUTY IN ALL SEASONS.

There's beauty all around us,
    On the land and on the sea,
In the tiny shell and pebble,
    In the leafy shrub and tree.
There's beauty all around us,
    In all seasons of the year,
When the clouds obscure the sunshine,
    And when the sky is clear.

There's beauty in the spring time
    When the fields are dressed anew,
In their garb of green all spangled
    With the little violets blue.
When grove and woodland echoes
    With the wild birds vesper song,
And the air is soft and balmy,
    As the zephyr sweeps along.

There's beauty in the summer,
    When the corn is in the ear,
When the rye is ripe and waving,
    And the curfew bells ring clear.
When bees their flight are winging,
    And the flowers bloom so gay,
When the earth its fruit is yielding,
    Oh! there's beauty every way.

There's beauty in the autumn,
Though it is of sadder tone,
Yet the evergreens are waving,
Though the birdies all have flown.
Autumn flowers lend their beauty
To the season's fading hours,
And the early frost gems sparkle
On each twig in leafless bowers.

There's beauty in the winter,
Though the chilly north winds blow,
When the sun is brightly shining
On the trees all draped in snow.
Then a thousand jewels glitter,
Wrought by winter's icy hand,
Yes, there's beauty in all seasons,
On the sea and on the land.

GRANDMOTHER'S STORY; OR, THE CHILD'S FAITH.

I am going to relate an incident that happened when I was a very little girl. My native place was Portsmouth in England; my parents had a large family of children, both boys and girls. I had an uncle and aunt come there to live; they had no children of their own, so they wanted to adopt one of us, but my mother said no, but I could live with them as long as they remained at Portsmouth. So I went and lived with aunt Dorothy, and I found her to be a very nice, pious woman. I well remember how pleasant we used to spend the evenings, when there was no company. Aunty would sing little hymns to me, and she had a music box which she would wind up and put on the table, for me to listen to. Once when we were alone sitting very quiet, she said suddenly to me, Bessie dear, if I should promise you a new doll to-morrow, would you feel sure of getting her?" I answered quickly "Yes, I'm sure I should, for you never tell me an untruth." "Now," said aunty, "I want you to understand that is what is meant by having faith, and I am very glad you have formed so good an opinion of me. Now I want to impress it on your mind that you must have faith in your Heavenly Father. When you are in trouble or want any thing that you are very desirous to obtain, you must fall on your knees and ask Him very earnestly for it, and if it is right and for your good, you will be sure to get what you ask for."

A few days after this conversation aunty told me if I was a good girl, and it was fine the next afternoon she would take me through the fair, and buy me a pretty work box.

Now, I was highly delighted at the prospect of going to the fair, and hoped it would be fine weather. As soon as I awoke the next morning I peeped out of the window, and oh! it rained. I felt very bad about it. Suddenly it came to my mind what aunty had said about faith, so I went right down on my knees, and said, "Please Lord to stop the rain and make it fine, so that aunty might take me to the fair." I rose up feeling quite sure that my prayer was heard and would be answered. About nine o'clock it ceased raining, and I could see patches of blue sky, and by ten o'clock the sun shone bright and clear. I remember that I felt very serious and thought what a good thing it is to have a Heavenly Father to ask to do what no earthly person can do for you. My faith then was very strong. The afternoon was very fine, and aunty and I had a pleasant walk through the fair, and I saw many beautiful things there. It was a large annual fair commencing on the 10th of July. It was free mart so there was a great many things for sale. I got my new work box and went home highly pleased with my day's adventure. Many years have passed since then and I am an old lady now, and have undergone many sorrows, but I have never forgotten my first faith; it has often prompted me in my trials to go to the fountain of all good.

LINES TO THE MEMORY OF MY COUSIN SARAH H. JARVIS.

Her spirit has flown to the mansions of rest,
Her feet are now treading the courts of the blest;
No more 'mid earth's toils and temptations to roam,
But resting in peace in her heavenly home.

She has passed on before to that beautiful land,
And taking her place 'mid the angelic band;
Her voice is now swelling their rapturous strain,
We would not recall her to sickness and pain.

Ah! no, though we miss the dear one who has gone,
We would not our darling to earth might return;
We would not imprison the spirit again,
Now free from life's trials and bodily pain.

We miss her at morning, we miss her at eve,
Ah, yes, we all miss her, yet we would not grieve;
But when we remember the days as of yore,
Our tears flow in silence—she's with us no more.

No more she will join in our innocent mirth,
We wept that so soon she must mingle with earth;
Soon flowers will blossom and over her wave,
And dews of the summer will moisten her grave.

Her voice always gentle—her smile and his kiss,
Her hand's kindly pressure, her love all we miss;
The form of our dear one is laid in the tomb,
But angels the spirit have bourn to their home.

The home of the ransomed so bright and so fair,
From earth she has gone all its glory to share;
She stands with the company of those robed in white,
They need not the sun or the moon to give light.

That country is lighted by radiance Divine,
The crowns of the ransomed the sun doth outshine;
And there dwells our loved one eternally blest,
No longer by sin and temptation oppressed.

And there we may meet her in that world above,
That city celestial the kingdom of love;
No parting tears fall in that blessed abode,
All those who meet there dwell forever with God.

Then farewell, dear Sarah, till time is no more,
Till we meet and greet thee on heaven's bright shore;
And join our glad voices in rapture to sing,
All honor and glory to Jesus our king.

ALMOST HOME.

As the good ship speeding on her homeward bound way draws near the end of a long and boisterous passage across the wide ocean, how the hearts of all on board thrill with joy as the cry of "Land ahead" is heard from the lookout aloft, every eye brightens and every voice echoes land ahead, and in a glad tone is added the soul-cheering words almost home. Many hasten into the rigging eager to catch a glimpse of the green shores of home, but land is too far away in the distance to be seen with the naked eye, and they are obliged to return to the deck to watch and wait encouraged with the thought of being almost home. In due time land is seen from the deck, then as the refreshing sight meets the eyes of the weary sailors, every heart and voice join in sending cheer after cheer, rolling far over the blue water. Flags are hoisted and the beaming countenance of each man as he hurries here and there as duty calls him, tells plainly that he is rejoicing in the thought of being almost home, and when a few hours after the good ship with flying colors glides gracefully into the harbor and drops anchor, she is greeted with loud cheers and a hearty welcome from those on shore, which is responded to by the now happy crew, and many a brave sailor as he again steps on his native shore, turns aside to brush away a tear of joy and gratitude, ere he grasps the hand of one and another of his old friends, who congratulate him on being again safe, safe at home. Thus it is with the Christian, who is drawing near the end of a long and tedious voyage across the ocean of life, as the ever green shore of eternity opens to view, joy unspeakable fills the soul, and the glorious thought of his heart finds utterance in the sweet words almost home, and when at last his frail barque glides smoothly into the harbor of heaven and cast anchor within the vale, he is greeted with cheers from the heavenly host, who gather on the golden strand to welcome him, and as his glorified spirit joins their number, there is wafted to us on a breeze from the celestial shore a faint echo of the joyful words, safe, safe at home.

PERSEVERANCE, OR THE FEEBLE ONE PROTECTED.

The scene described in the following poem was witnessed by a lady who, in a desponding state of mind, was walking early one morning along the sea shore on the Isle of Wight, England.

> I wandered forth at early morn,
>   As I had often done before;
> With gloomy thoughts I strayed alone,
>   Along the pebbled sandy shore.
>
> My heart was sad by doubt oppressed,
>   My mind disturbed by anxious fear;
> My weary spirit longed for rest,
>   I sighing, dropped a silent tear.
>
> A stormy wind swept o'er the deep,
>   And deafening was the tempest roar;
> As surge on surge in fury leap,
>   And wreaked their vengeance on the shore.
>
> As I the troubled scene surveyed,
>   A flock of sea birds floated by;
> The storm their voyage had not delayed,
>   I watched them with an earnest eye.
>
> They boldly stemmed the fearful gale,
>   Without a compass or a chart;
> Guided by instinct on they sail,
>   For distant lands they now depart.
>
> But one, perhaps a feeble one,
>   Appears to faint and weary grow;
> Now slowly flies along alone,
>   While swiftly on the others go.
>
> And lower, lower still he drops,
>   Till now upon an ocean wave,
> To gather strength the weak one stops,
>   Then all alone the storm to brave.

He rises on the wing again,
  His lonely journey to pursue;
He slowly passes o'er the main,
  And now is hidden from my view.

Poor bird, I said, thy fate is sealed,
  Thy pinions cease to bear thee on;
Thy strength and courage, too, has failed,
  And weary thou art left alone.

But suddenly I saw him rise,
  In rapid flight and soaring high;
With strength renewed he swiftly flies,
  To join his comrades far away.

Then slowly I my steps retraced,
  My gloomy thoughts and anxious fears
To faith and peace had given place;
  My eyes overflowed with grateful tears.

He who doth mark the sparrows fall,
  Will not forsake the feeble one;
He stoops to hear us when we call,
  To Him our wants and fears are known.

Though years have passed since on that morn,
  I watched the sea bird in his flight;
Then humbled by the scene, I learned
  To trust a Saviour's love and might.

THE ACORN AND THE OAK.

One day a good many years ago, an acorn fell into a hollow in the ground. It was soon covered with dry leaves and dust, and after a while the hollow was filled up and the little acorn was buried several inches below the surface. It lay very quiet for a long time; bye and bye when spring opened the acorn began to get restless—a desire to climb upward took possession of it. It was cold and dark down there and very lonely. Day by day it grew more restless, and the desire to climb upward grew stronger. At last in a desperate struggle it burst its shell; this was a happy release. Now I am free thought the acorn. I will climb up and see what I can see, so it climbed and climbed, and early one morning two little leaves peeped out of the ground; they appeared fresh and green, and looked as if they might be saying, "What a big world this is, and how pleasant it is. I am so glad we have got up into the beautiful light of day." Pretty soon the sun rose, shining bright and warm on the tiny plant, making its heart dance for joy. As day advanced the rays of the sun grew stronger; noon came and passed, and afternoon was waning. The air was hot and dry and the little plant feeling weary began to query, "How shall I get water to drink? I am very thirsty. If the sun always shines so brightly I shall be scorched to death. I wonder how those great trees get a drink; they are so very large while I am very small. Surely when water is given them I shall not be forgotten." In due time the sun went down, and as the shades of night drew on, dew began to fall, cooling the air and reviving nature. Every large tree and each small blade of grass received its share of the refreshing moisture. All night the baby oak sipped the cool dew drops, and when morning dawned it hailed the rising sun with new strength and vigor. Days and nights came and went, weeks and months passed away, and the young oak gathered strength from sunshine and from shower. Several years went by and the tiny plant had grown to be a small tree, nodding its head and waving its branches in the breeze and anticipating the pleasure it would realize when it became a large oak. And, when for the first time a bird lighted upon one of its limbs, that small tree was just as proud as a small tree could be. Time went on and years rolled around, and one day in summer an old man and a little boy came and sat under the shadow of a great oak. The old man said to the little boy, "I remember well when this large tree was quite small, and now we can sit under the shade of its long branches." Just then a rustling was heard, and the old man and the boy thought a light breeze stirred the leaves, but it was the tree laughing, pleased and happy to know that at last it was numbered among the great trees of the woods where it grew, affording shade and shelter to man and birds.

MORNING MEDITATIONS.

When we awake in the morning the first thoughts that take possession of the mind should be those that give rise to feelings of deep gratitude to God for his merciful protection through the dark and silent hours of the past night. Most assuredly at all times and in all places we need the all powerful arm of God to defend and protect us, but while unconscious in sweet repose we are indeed depending on the kind care of our Heavenly Father, for then it is however near danger may be to us we know it not; consequently, we are powerless to help ourselves unless aroused to consciousness by the interposition of Providence. Oh! what a comfort it is to know there is one who never slumbers, never grows weary, and who is almighty to preserve us unharmed through dangers seen and unseen, by night as well as by day. Oh! what a blessing to awake in the morning with bodily strength renewed, energy refreshed and in full possession of health, and all the faculties with which God has endowed us, for those favors we should be especially thankful. While we lay peacefully sleeping, undisturbed by pain or even an ill dream, many have been tossing on a bed of sickness, with parched lips and fevered brow from whose eyelids sleep had fled, and who weary of the long and tedious night have wished for morning. Others poor and needy have not a comfortable bed to lie upon, but vainly try to rest their weary limbs on a pallet of straw, with little or no covering save the dark curtain of night, and but poorly sheltered. Others again more destitute have not even a place of shelter, but wander about the streets until, overcome by exposure and fatigue, they sink down in some corner and sleep, or more properly speaking, became unconscious from sheer exhaustion. When we consider those things we can truly say, "Not more than others I deserve, yet God has given me more." Poor though we may feel ourselves to be in wordly things, yet we are surrounded by comforts that many poor creatures never know. What have we done to merit such favor more than they? What are we that God is mindful of us? Yet how seldom do we pause to meditate upon his tender goodness and the manifold blessings bestowed upon us, sinful as we are and unworthy of the least of them. Had God been strict to have marked one sin in a thousand we might now have been reaping the reward of misspent years. While we slept, the silver cord of life might have been broken, and we suddenly ushered into eternity; and if we had sank to slumber unprepared for that awful event how fearful to think of the consequence. But God remembers our frailty and deals with us not according to our iniquities, but according to the wondrous love and kindness of His compassionate nature; for He wills not the death of a sinner, but rather that every one should turn to Him and live. Therefore, He bears with our infirmities and spares us from day to day and from time to time, living monuments of His tender mercy. Yet how often do we slight our Father's love and grieve His holy spirit by weakly yielding to wrong. How often do we stray far out of the narrow path, lured by the pomp and vanity of this world, at times seeming to forget that this is not our abiding place. Oh! let us remember life is but short, our days are as the grass, which flourisheth in the morning and in the evening it is cut down. Let us try faithfully and constantly to do the will of our Heavenly Father, and if we strive to walk in the way He has marked out for us, earnestly seeking His aid and guidance and humbly asking for a continuance of His favor, He is merciful to forgive our shortcomings, blot out our transgressions and lead us safely on through the dark and uneven journey of life, and at last give us a place in His kingdom above. Thus, with soul refreshed by prayer and meditation, even as the summer rain refresheth the dry and thirsty earth, we go forth cheerfully to the duties of the day with grateful heart and songs of praise prepared alike for trials and for triumphs.

EVENING MEDITATIONS.

When day has passed and the shades of evening fall around us like a curtain, before retiring to rest for the night, we should devote at least a few moments to meditation. While thus engaged we cannot fail to recognize the watchful care of our all-wise creator and guardian in bringing us safely to the close of another day—still in the enjoyment of health and favorable circumstances. Oh! what a blessing to be able to say it is well with us. No bitter disappointment disturbs our thoughts; no sudden grief filling the heart with sorrow, and no new burden of care or trouble weighing heavily upon the mind. Humbly thankful that we are free from these great trials, we lay aside with feelings of gratitude ones of less weight and shutting out the

world from our thoughts for a time, quietly reflect on
the love and kindness of our Heavenly Father, and the
many blessings He has bestowed upon us, which we
daily and hourly enjoy. Truly the goodness and mercy
of God has followed us all the days of our lives even
until the present moment, yet how often do we prove
unmindful of His favors. The world and worldly things
beloved our anxious thoughts employ. How faint and
cold is our love to God in return for His love so abundant
to us, and how often, oh! how often do we pray to and
praise Him with our lips, while our hearts are far
from Him. Oh! let us solemnly remember that God
will not accept such soulless prayers, for He requires
those who worship Him to worship Him in spirit and
in truth. Therefore, let us consider our ways and take
heed to our steps, lest we fall and there be none to help
us in the hour of need. Oh! let us strive to live so that
each day as it passeth may be a day's journey nearer
heaven. By God's grace we have been strengthened in
the hour of temptation and thus enabled to resist and
overcome the tempter. Had we depended on our own
strength it would have proved utterly insufficient, and
weak and feeble we would have fallen an early prey to
the enemy of our souls. But He who says My grace is
sufficient for you, hath delivered us from all evil. How
often in time past have we been shielded from danger
by the protecting arm of God. Not on account of our
own righteousness or worthiness were we saved from
sudden destruction, but because of the compassionate
forbearance and pitying love of God He has spared
us a little longer, that we may see the error of our
ways, and seek to be more faithful in the service of

our Lord and Master. By the infinite goodness of God we have been provided with food enough and to spare; our daily bread is supplied with a bountiful hand; cold and hunger are privations of which we know nothing. We are sheltered in a peaceful, pleasant home, surrounded by many comforts, from which when we go forth we are warmly clad and covered from the cold. We dwell in a land of peace and plenty, undisturbed by the din of battle and fearing no famine, because the Lord has blessed the labors of the husbandman, filling his barns with rich harvests. While the daily needs of the body are thus being supplied, the soul is also as abundantly provided for. We live in an age and in a country glorious with the light and liberty of the true Gospel of Jesus Christ. All may enjoy the privileges and blessings of Christianity, worshipping God at home or in the sanctuary, unmolested and without fear or persecution, because the precious fountain of God's love and pardon flows free to all. Truly ours is a goodly heritage. When we consider what a favored lot is ours, the heart melts in fervent gratitude to God, the author of our being, and all the advantages we every day enjoy both temporal and spiritual. Thus with renewed confidence in the love and care of our Heavenly Father, we by prayer commit ourselves in child-like faith to His keeping, then retire to rest and sweetly sleep at peace with God and man.

THE RUINED CITY.

The following poem was composed after hearing a book read entitled "Petra, or the Rocky City." This book contains an interesting description of the ruins of an ancient and once magnificent city, the capital of Idumea in the Holy Land.

No more thy merry bells send forth
    Their joyous peal at set of sun,
No more is heard the sound of mirth
    At all, in thee deserted one.

No more the sound of revelry
    Shall wake the silence of thy halls,
No more shall scenes of gayety
    Be witnessed by those crumbling walls.

A gloomy hush doth thee enshroud,
    Thy pomp and grandeur gone for aye,
Homes of the rich, the gay, the proud,
    Are slowly sinking to decay.

Thy streets, where once the motley throng
    Were seen to hurry to and fro,
Where stately chariots rolled along,
    Are filled with thorns and thistles now.

Thy noble mansions that once stood
    In dazzling splendor to behold,
Now seem to mourn in solitude;
    Like caves, within are damp and cold.

Thy domes and spires are broken down,
    Thy pride lies humbled in the dust,
And ruined splendor all around
    Shows what in days before thou wast.

Through distant lands was heard thy fame,
    Thou noble city of the past,
Hither the wandering stranger came,
    Not then to say as now, alas!

But now thou art left all alone,
In death-like silence to decay,
Scarcely a stone left on a stone,
Thy glory all has past away.

Alas! 'tis thus, we know not why,
Yet we lament thy awful fate,
We turn from thee, but with a sigh,
And leave thee lone and desolate.

THE ISLANDS OF THE BAY OF FUNDY.

The Bay of Fundy contains three hundred and sixty-five islands, including quite a number of rocks. Those rocks or ledges are so various in size that while some are standing high out of the water, many appear just above, and others level with the surface, making the Bay very dangerous and difficult to navigate. So much so that even skillful and experienced pilots do not always succeed in getting vessels in or out of the Bay in safety. The most prominent features of those islands are long, sandy shores, coves and creeks, high cliffs and lofty hills, with here and there a running brook or bubbling spring, affording a bounteous supply of clear, pure water. Some of the islands are quite large, while others are very small. The trees growing on them are for the most part spruce and fir, with a few pine, cedar and birch; there are also some hemlock and dogwood trees. The dogwood tree grows as near the bank as it can safely stand, and in autumn is heavily laden with large clusters of red berries. Those after being touched with the first light frost of early winter are very pleasant to eat. The soil produces a great variety of wild berries, such as strawberries, raspberries, cranberries and many other berries too numerous to mention. Some of the outer islands are uninhabited, save by the feathered tribe. There, undisturbed, the crow, the hawk and the eagle have their homes in the thick woods, while the sea fowls collect in large numbers on the shores, and make their nests in the bank.

On the beaches in different parts of the Bay there are some very large and curiously shaped rocks; among the rest is one so closely resembling a man with a hat and gown on, that it is called the Bishop. Another is called the Bull-dog, it being very much like that animal in appearance. Strangers who visit the island during the summer seasons are delighted with the freshness and beauty of the scenery. There they escape the dust and heat of town and city, and enjoy the cool sea breeze. From the summit of some of the loftier hills a fine prospect is presented to the eye, and a walk of a mile or two never fails to please and interest visitors.

The inhabitants of the islands are as a rule an industrious, cheerful, hospitable and intelligent people. For a livelihood they depend chiefly on fishing. Those who can afford to do so keep what fish they catch during the summer and in the fall take them to market altogether, taking up part of the price they bring in trade and return home with their winter's supply of groceries and fishing gear, and in some cases a well filled purse.

When a young man starts in life, or goes on his own

hook as they say, the first thing he gets is a fishing boat and herring net or two. Some of the more prosperous fishermen own a small vessel and five or six nets; the average length of these nets are about sixty fathoms and valued at fifty dollars. The fish houses, smoke houses and sheds, in which the fish are cured and stored for market, stand in rows on the shore, a safe distance above high water mark, and in summer these, together with the scores of men and boys engaged in taking care of the fish, present a lively appearance.

In the fall, at an appointed time, there is what is called the race day. In the forenoon a fish fair is held, in the afternoon there is a boat race, and in the evening a supper is served, after which the remainder of the night is spent in dancing. At these annual exhibitions there are to be seen some very fine specimens of the different kinds of fish caught in the Bay, herrings, mackerel, codfish, pollock and haddock. Those who win the prizes on their fish or in the boat race are highly gratified. Almost every married man owns the house he lives in, and not less than two or three acres of land, raises his own vegetables, keeps a cow, a few sheep, a pig and some poultry. The women, besides attending to their household affairs, milk the cows, spin the yarn, and net the herring nets. When the wild berries are in season they go out in small parties and gather them to preserve for winter use. The houses are all frame buildings, some of them quite large and pretty. Each village has its church and on Sunday the people make a very respectable appearance. There are but two sects, the Episcopal and Baptist. The Bay of Fundy was many years ago the rendezvous of a band of sea robbers, headed by the famous pirate Captain Kidd, and a better place for concealment could hardly be found, for there some of the harbors are so formed that a vessel might sail up and by turning a bend be completely hidden, while those unacquainted with the navigation of the Bay would never suspect the hiding place.

In a large cove on the south east side of the island of Campobello there is what is said to be the remains of a pirate ship. When the tide is out the ends of the timbers are to be seen standing out of the mud in which the hull is imbedded. The wreck is probably resting on a rock and will there remain perhaps for ages, as the wood of which the vessel was built is oak. Near the same cove there is said to be a hogshead of money buried. The money was left by pirates in the care of a man named Dunbar. His wife, taking advantage of his absence for a day or two, buried the money. On his return she refused to tell him where she had hidden it; he grew angry with her; from words they came to blows, until at last, he being the stronger of the two overpowered and killed her. He was arrested, tried, condemned and was the first man hung in the town of St. Andrew's, New Brunswick. The exact spot where the money was buried has never yet been discovered. On another island called Casco there is said to be a chest of money buried. The spot is easily found, for every night from dark until daylight, a bright light is to be seen on the place where the treasure is supposed to be hidden. More than once the ground has been disturbed by parties trying to get possession of it, but none as yet have succeeded.

Tradition says that when Captain Kidd was about to bury money he always had one of his men killed and laid beside the treasure to take care of it. One moonlight night in summer, three men well known to the writer were digging for the money on Casco Island, silence being the order. After working for some time one of their spades came in contact with what was supposed to be the iron chest, but no one spoke. After a short time the sound was repeated; still silence was maintained. In a few minutes more when, for the third time the iron was struck, a groaning was heard, accompanied by a strong smell of sulphur. The chap who had charge of that money was evidently beginning to fear he would be overpowered, and was signaling for help, for just at that moment a slight noise in the distance caused the men to look up, when lo and behold! a full rigged pirate ship was gliding swiftly round a headland of the island. When it came opposite the spot where the men were the anchor was dropped, and a great noise was heard on board as if many men were preparing to land. Our friends did not wait to see whether they landed or not, but hastily leaving the spot, quickly made their way to the boat and hurried home.

The next day they told the story of their adventure, declaring it to be a fact. We do not for a moment doubt the veracity of those men, neither do we presume to say they had no grounds for their assertion, for it would not be an unusual occurrence for a vessel to drop anchor near the island, while waiting for wind or tide, and should such happen just at that time and place, it would be easy for the already excited imagination of the men to conjure even a small vessel into something more formidable. A great deal of pirate money is supposed to be buried on different islands of the Bay of Fundy. Doubtless there is, but if Captain Kidd takes as good care of it all as he does of the chest on Casco Island, it would be of but little use to any one to know where it is hidden.

ARTHUR TO NANCY.

Yes, well do I remember
    The day when first we met;
Those scenes of youth's bright morning
    I never can forget.
Thy hair now white as silver,
    Then fell in soft brown curls,
My little blue eyed Nancy
    Reigned queen among the girls.

Thy cheeks now pale and furrowed,
    Then bloomed like roses red,
And smiles of youthful gladness
    O'er thy sweet face was shed.
And oft in twilight hours
    Through smiling fields we've strayed,
Or wandered by the woodland,
    Beneath the silent shade.

The day I claimed thee, Nancy,
    To be my happy bride,
They strewed the way with flowers,
    I looked on thee with pride.
With pride I saw them weaving
    A crown for thy fair brow,
Of bright and blooming roses,
    But they are faded now.

Yet you and I, dear Nancy,
    Still journey hand in hand,
We've seen our children's children
    Around our hearthstone stand.
When other hearts did fail me
    Thy counsel was my guide,
And dark would be life's journey
    Without thee by my side.

THE DISCOMFITED LOVER.

Mr. Pratt was the new school master in the village, boarding at the house of Mrs. Willes. One Sunday afternoon Mrs. Willes was accompanied home from church by a widow lady, an acquaintance of hers who lived a couple of miles from the village. The widow was young, lively and pretty, and so it was no wonder that Mr. Pratt, who was a widower, was not slow to fall in love with her. In the evening of the following day, as that gentleman sat looking thoughtfully out of the window, apparently engaged in the task of counting the leaves on the trees growing in the front of the house, Mrs. Willes asked him what he was thinking about, but before he could answer she added, "I bet my snuff box you are thinking of the widow." "You're right," said he. "Well," said she, "go and propose to her and let us have a wedding." "I do not know that she would have me," was his reply. "Nor you never will know, if you do not ask her," said Mrs. Willes, and she added by way of encouragement, "a faint heart never won a fair lady." "Exactly," said he, "I will go and see her next Saturday." During the week Mrs. Willes managed to see the widow and apprise her of the intended visit. Saturday came and with it came Mr. Pratt dressed in his best. He was shown into the parlor, where sat the widow and a Mrs. Gray, a lady visitor. It was not long before he discovered that Mrs. Gray was slightly dull of hearing, and after a little time spent in general conversation, he approached the subject uppermost in his mind by saying, "It is quite an advantage, Mrs. Gray being dull of hearing." "Advantage," repeated the widow somewhat sharply, "Advantage, I think it a great disadvantage." "Ah, yes, to her of course," said Mr. Pratt, his face turning as red as a boiled lobster. "But—but," he continued, "I, I—came to have a little private talk with you." "You need not say anything to me that you do not wish Mrs. Gray to hear," said the widow. "But," said the gentleman, much agitated and wiping the perspiration from his brow with a large silk handkerchief, "I—I—came to ask you to be my wife." "You might have saved yourself the trouble, for I will not," was the decided answer of the widow. Mr. Pratt arose, highly indignant, and replied as he hastily advanced towards the door, "There is many a lady as young and as pretty as you, who would be glad of the offer you have rejected to-day." So saying he closed the door with a bang, and hurried from the house. He had not gone far when, to his dismay, he discovered that in his excitement he had come away without his hat. What should he do. He would not go back for it, if he had to go home bare headed; neither would he send for it if he never got it, and what excuse could he make if any one should ask him what had become of his hat. While those perplexing thoughts were running through his mind he had unconsciously slackened his pace and was walking quite slow, when he heard hasty footsteps behind him, and on looking back he saw a little girl coming with his hat. He waited for her to come up, seized the hat, and without saying a word, placed it on his head with so much force as to almost cause rim and crown to part company, and resumed his walk with rapid strides. On reaching home Mrs. Willes, pretending not to notice the look of disappointment plainly visible on his countenance, asked him good naturedly how he had "succeeded." "Succeeded," said he, "I wish I had never seen her."

THE ROSE.

The rosebud is gently unfolding its leaves,
   Perfuming the air with its breath,
Now graceful it waves in the soft summer breeze,
   But soon it will slumber in death.

Yes, short is thy stay on thy stem, blushing rose,
   You will wave in the breeze but a day,
Ere the dew shall fall at the twilight's close,
   Thy beauty shall vanish away.

Ere the sun shall sink in the far distant west,
   Ere his last lingering ray has fled,
Thou queen of the flowers, thou fairest and best,
   Thy leaves will be scattered and dead.

Thus man doth appear like the rose of to-day,
   Time glides like a still flowing stream,
The years roll along and refuse to stay,
   Man passes away like a dream.

A WELCOME TO SPRING.

Cold winter is gone with his ice and his snow,
And hushed are the rude winds that fiercely did blow,
Fair spring has returned with her soft frequent gales,
That steal o'er the mountains and sigh through the vales.

How gladly we hail the return of the spring,
Fair prospects, gay sunshine, her presence doth bring;
The fields are arrayed in their verdure once more,
Good bye to cold winter and rude tempests roar.

The streamlets go singing and murmuring on,
They seem to rejoice that the winter is gone;
And nature has spread her soft carpet again
Of emerald green over valley and plain.

Away through the fields to the hill tops repair,
In the bright rosy morning, and breathe the fresh air,
And join with the birds in full chorus to greet
The beautiful spring time so balmy and sweet.

Fresh beauty is scattered profusely around,
All nature springs into new life at a bound;
The lambs skip and sport in their frolicsome glee,
The birds and the beasts seem as happy as we.

The earth seems to smile and the sky looks so blue,
We feel as if life was beginning anew;
The aged and young all rejoice to behold
The beautiful spring its rare treasures unfold.

A voice softly whispers be grateful to God,
Who pours out his blessings so freely abroad;
Then gratitude flows from our hearts as we sing,
And hail with delight the bright beautiful spring.

MEMORY.

Memory paints pictures and hangs them in the chambers of the mind; time cannot efface them. If it were not so, life would be a void and cheerless. For how often in after years does the spirit seem to wander through those chambers, lingering lovingly over the fair pictures of the past. None are left out or unfinished; all are complete and in their proper places. First, there are those of innocent childhood, seen in a clear, soft, rosy light, the blithe forms and smiling faces of playmates, merry Christmas gatherings, and pretty toys, happy school days, and beautiful spring time; little figures robed in white, kneeling with hands clasped at mother's knee, or by the trundle bed offering the evening prayer; holy Sabbath days and dear old grandparents, long since gone to their rest. All are faithfully painted by memory. Then there are scenes of youth, forms more noble and graceful, faces still smiling, but more matured and wreathed with hopes, bright flowers just opening into bloom, social gatherings and pleasant walks, pleasing incidents and beautiful prospects, the forming of new ties and acquaintances, visits to foreign lands, and days of public rejoicings; all these and many others are studied with never flagging interest. And again there are pictures more touchingly beautiful, deeds of kindness, making glad the hearts of the needy, the reunion of kindred after a long separation, a pleasant home and the fair, innocent face, and white dimpled hands of an infant, a troop of noisy happy children, the joy of seeing those children grow up to be useful and worthy members of society, the conversion of a wife or husband, the reclaiming of sons and daughters from the paths of sin and folly, by those the spirit loves to linger, and forgetful of the present seems to live again in the past. There are also scenes of sadness, for in no case is memory spared the task of painting those. Adversity and disappointments, parting with loved ones and leaving native country to dwell in a distant land among strangers, a darling child placed in the coffin, a dear sister or brother cold in death, a beloved father or mother, perhaps both, laid low in the valley, or it may be the chosen companion of youth gone on before. After gazing on these scenes with tear dimmed eyes and saddened heart, the spirit draws a curtain over them and turns away in mournful silence. As the body advances in years memory becomes less busy, the things of to-day are noticed only to be forgotten by to-morrow, and as life closes the pencil drops from memory's hand, and the spirit passes from earth to dwell in a world where there is no past, no future, but one continual present time swallowed up in eternity.

HOW THE PASSAMAQUODDY INDIANS
WIN THEIR BRIDES.

When a young man sees a young woman he thinks he would like as a partner for life, he watches her for a time with a jealous eye, but never ventures to speak to her, for the young men and maidens of that tribe have no intercourse with each other. When he is quite sure she is just the style that suits, he goes to her guardian, her father if he is living, and asks for her to be his wife. The person thus applied to tells the maiden of the request and by whom it has been made. A ball is immediately gotten up, all interested in the affair are invited, and at the appointed time the guests arrive, music and dancing begins, and all goes merry as a marriage bell. The music consists in rattling a handful of shot in a powder horn or flask. Each dancer takes one in his hand, and as they dance and sing the shot is rattled to the tune. After the amusement is fairly begun, the young lover approaches the object of his affection and with hope and fear striving in his heart, asks her to dance with him. If she does not wish to become his wife she signifies the same by refusing to dance, and the poor fellow, disappointed, hurries away from the place, and the assembly disperse at an early hour. On the other hand, if he finds favor in her eyes, she appears as his partner in the dance. The happy couple are immediately united in the holy bands of matrimony and the merry-making is continued for several days.

TO A FRIEND ABOUT TO CROSS THE OCEAN.

You are going far away,
    May you soon your haven gain,
We will think of you each day
    When you're out upon the main.

O'er the ocean, wide and deep,
    May your bark in safety glide,
Wide awake or fast asleep
    May no danger you betide.

May no stormy winds arise,
    No dark threatening clouds hang low,
Fair above you be the skies,
    And may gentle breezes blow.

Should the tempest wake the deep,
    And the angry billows roar,
Heaven guard and safe you keep
    From the storm-king's mighty power.

Well and safely may you land
    On Brittania's sea-washed shore,
Press again your native strand,
    Tread old England's soil once more.

There with friends and kindred dear,
    May the time pass happily,
When remembering others here,
    Will you kindly think of me.

MY MOTHER'S STORY ABOUT HER BIBLE.

(As related by Herself.)

My husband was of a very lively disposition and extremely fond of company, and as is usual, it caused him to be fond of the social glass. He was not what might be called a drunkard, but he would sometimes take one more than he could conveniently carry. He was a sea-faring man, and was for some time mate of a large ship called the *John and Mary*, belonging to Sunderland, a seaport town in the north of England. The ship did not make long voyages; she often went no farther than London. Once when my husband was about to sail for London, I asked him if he would please go to the Bible Society's rooms and buy me a nice sized Bible. I told him he could get a large one there for the same price he would have to give elsewhere for a small one. He said he would try and think of it. I thought no more on the subject until my husband came home again. I then asked him if he had brought my Bible. He answered no, "I took some money ashore to buy you one, but went the wrong road." He said, "I met a friend and we had a little spree together." I cannot express how bad I felt as my dear young husband stood there, telling me that he had taken the money which he had intended to buy a Bible with, to have a little spree as he called it. My heart was so full that, leaning my head upon his shoulder, I wept. He also shed tears. After a little while he said to me, "Why, what is the matter? I did not think you were such a baby. Never mind, if the Lord spares me to go to London again I will bring you a Bible." About a week after the ship sailed for London, as my husband was going out of the door, I whispered in his ear don't forget your promise. He answered, "God helping me I will not forget it." I put on my bonnet and went down to see the ship leave the harbor. I watched her far out upon the water, then I returned home, went up stairs and kneeling down by the side of the bed, I prayed earnestly to my Heavenly Father that He would make my dear husband a good Christian man, and also give him grace and strength to keep his promise.

It was usual for the *John and Mary* to be three weeks on a voyage to London and back, but she had been gone only a little over two weeks when, one evening I heard my husband's footsteps passing the window. I hastened and met him at the door. I said, "You have come before I expected you." He answered, "watch, for ye know not the day or the hour when the Son of Man cometh." I was surprised, knowing that in all his worldly ways he never scoffed at religion. So I asked him what he meant. He told me the Lord had done great things for him; He had made him a new man. "Let us sit down and I will tell you all about it." I noticed that he had a parcel under his arm, which he laid on the table, and we sat down by the cheerful coal fire, he then began by saying, "Your feeling so hurt at my not bringing your Bible made me very uneasy whilst home, and as soon as we arrived in London, I heard there was a great revival going on in the Primitive Methodist Church; so in the evening Mr. Boyce and I went ashore and found the church. The people had a glorious time, and I ventured up amongst the rest to be prayed for. After we came out of church we went on board our ship. I did not sleep much that night; I got up several times and knelt down, but could not pray. The next day I went about my duty as usual, and in the evening we went again to the church, and bless the Lord, He pardoned all my sins and I am a new creature."

After I had expressed my joy at the great change that had taken place in him, he took the parcel from the table, and after taking off the wrapper, he presented to me my new Bible. It was a nice morocco bound book; the leaves were gilt edged. After examining and making our comments on the outside, we opened the book and found that it was printed in a nice, clear type. We then read several chapters, each reading a verse by turn. That night my husband erected the family altar, which was never broken until he was laid up by his last sickness. The next week he joined a temperance society, called the Rechabites, and as long as he lived he was a strict upholder of temperance principles. I have my Bible yet; I have had it forty years. It is well worn and looks a little shabby, the gilt is all gone from the edges, but I prize it, yes, I prize it very highly, and would not part with it for the most costly one that could be purchased.

GOD SEEN IN ALL HIS WORKS.

How wond'rous are the works of God,
  In wisdom hath he wrought them all,
Earth was created at His word,
  Sun, moon and stars came at His call,
When darkness was upon the earth
  God spoke and said let there be light,
The light appeared, He called it day,
  Also the darkness He called night.

God spake again, the waters fled,
  A pace from off the earth, then stayed;
The mighty ocean knew its bounds,
  Its Maker's mandate was obeyed,
God spoke and verdure clothed the fields,
  The trees did yield abundant food,
He saw the works His word had wrought,
  And blessed them and pronounced them good.

The birds, the beasts, the fishes all
  Came in obedience to His word.
And were submissive to His will,
  Each took their place and knew their Lord,
When man God formed out of the dust,
  In his own likeness man He made,
And placed him in fair Eden's bowers,
  Where oft they met at evening shade.

Oh! who can sound the deep abyss,
  Of such amazing power and skill,
Oh! who can solve God's mysteries
  And understand His righteous will,
When mortals pause awhile and think,
  And contemplate the vast design,
Deep reverence doth possess the soul,
  And awe and wonder fill the mind.

The sun that rules as king of day,
The moon and stars that shine afar,
Their Maker's glory all show forth,
And they His wisdom do declare.
The tiny blades of grass that form,
The rich green carpet of the earth,
These seem to softly whispering say,
'Twas tender goodness gave us birth.

The flowers that bloom in varied hues,
Adorning hill and dale and grove,
These all in silent eloquence
Proclaim to us that God is love.
Behold the giant forest trees,
Like faithful sentinels they stand,
Their wild majestic beauty reigns,
Preserved and fostered by God's hand.

The birds in tuneful chorus join
To praise the Lord for blessings given,
Their music cheers man in his toil,
And upward turns his thoughts to heaven,
The bee, the butterflies, the ant,
Tell us of God's unfailing care,
Each little shrub and every plant
Show us that God is everywhere.

The mountain and the prairie wide,
The lofty hill, the lowly dell,
The lake, the river and the brook,
Of their creator's goodness tell.
All upward look and seem to say,
God made us and His name we praise,
He doth supply our every need,
Bless Him, for wondrous are His ways.

Out on the ocean wide is seen,
God's mighty works upon the deep,
When gloomy darkness doth enshroud
And weary watch the sailors keep,

When mountain billows fiercely foam,
   And tempests rage with fearful power,
Man, trembling, bows his head and owns
   God's presence in that awful hour.

And when the storm has passed away,
   The waves subdued, the tempest staid,
Stilled by a word from Him whose power
   O'er all is then and there displayed.
Earth, sea and sky, all, all proclaim
   Their Maker's wondrous love and skill,
And all unite to praise His name,
   And each their mission do fulfil.

What wondrous love, what tender care,
   Unerring wisdom, power supreme,
Justice and judgment righteous pure,
   In all the works of God are seen.
Join all the universe to sing
   His praise, who doeth all things well,
Join every creature here below,
   Loud let the grateful anthem swell.

FRETTING WITHOUT CAUSE.

There are individuals in almost every community who, though they are surrounded with every comfort they can reasonably desire, yet their chief aim in life seems to be to keep themselves and every body around them as unhappy as possible. They delight only in finding fault and fretting over it. They are hard to please and easy to offend; they cannot speak to a neighbor without recounting their troubles past and present, and even presuming to borrow largely from the future. If a friend calls in to spend a few minutes with them, they take up the whole time in telling their grievances; in fact they are always fretting over their troubles, their constant complaining wearies those with whom they associate. The consequence is their society is shunned rather than sought after. They do not enjoy life as they might, because they look only on the dark side, positively refusing to see bright spots even when they are pointed out to them. They receive the good gifts of Providence with dissatisfied feelings, as though they thought the blessings bestowed upon them did not by half make up for what they were denied.

It may well be said of them they gather together all the troubles within their reach, make them up into one great burden and, bending their backs to the self-imposed task, take the burden on their shoulders and move along the path of life at a slow pace, wearing a dejected look and keeping up a continual sing song about their troubles. They expect the sympathy of every one, while they themselves have but little or none for others. To such as these we would say with all due respect, "Friend, lay down your burden and examine the contents." We think on inspection you will find a great part is made up of imaginary troubles. There are also quite a number you have borrowed from next week or next month, and even next year; leave all those, take only those which you are obliged to and you will be astonished to find how much lighter your burden is; so much so, that you will feel quite happy; and what will help to keep it light is to remember that your troubles are but small compared with those of many others. Think of the invalid enduring months and years of suffering; think of those who are called upon by death to give up one loved one after another, until the cup of grief runneth over; think of the blind, the deaf mute and the cripple; think of the poor and the needy, who suffer cold and hunger; think of all those and then consider your own favorable circumstances, and pour out your heart in thankfulness to God for the manifold blessings you enjoy. Your general health is good, you are surrounded by those who are near and dear to you, you have the full free use of all your faculties and limbs, your daily food is bountifully supplied, and you suffer not for raiment; why then grieve your Heavenly Father with ingratitude and make yourself miserable by fretting without a cause. Do not anticipate trouble, leave things of the future alone; the present only is yours; many of those troubles seen at a distance will disappear altogether and others become much less should you live to meet them. Do not fret over slight troubles for they are strewn plentifully in the path of every one, but daily experience teaches us that whining and worrying will neither remove nor lessen them, but only tends to make them a great deal worse. Go through or around them as quietly as possible. Even though it takes a little more time it will pay you in the end, if you only succeed in preserving your peace of mind and pleasant countenance. It will be hard at first, but persevere; each victory will make the next easier, and as you gain ground you will win the love and respect of all who know you, so that should the hour of adversity come or you be called to bow beneath the chastening rod of affliction, you will find many sympathizing and true friends. Do not depend on your own strength to overcome your besetting sin, look to Him who says, "My grace is sufficient for you." Believe Him, trust Him and all will be well.

SHAMMING INSANITY.

(Written by Mother.)

Many years ago I had an uncle who belonged to the British army. He was always allowed a man servant, and I well remember two of them. The name of the first one was Tom Plant. I heard my uncle say it was rumored that he belonged to a wealthy family, but had incurred their displeasure by being very wild, and he had joined the army, thinking it an easy way of getting a livelihood, but as he was tired of it, he was then shamming insanity for the purpose of getting his discharge, and he acted it well while he was with my uncle. He would go about stooping like an old man, though he was quite a youth.

One day my aunt and I happened to be in the pantry when Tom brought in a dish of fish he had been cleaning, he placed the dish on the floor, under a hook he intended to hang them on, and holding it there awhile he then took a few steps backwards, ran at the dish again and clutching it with both hands, gave it a good shaking; he went through this manoeuvre several times. When I said, "Tom, what are you shaking the dish so for," he looked at me with a broad grin on his face and answered, "Why, miss, I am shaking the dish to make it sit firm." Aunty said she "thought it would sit firm enough now," so he took the fish and hanging them on the hook stepped back as before. After gazing at the fish awhile he spring at them and clasping them around with both hands, shook them with such force that the string broke, and the fish slipping from his grasp flew in all directions. My aunt and I left the pantry laughing heartily; Tom laughed too, as I suppose, at seeing the fish flying round him. He would act the same by everything he used. If he had been sweeping, he would place the broom in a corner and hold it there, giving it sundry jerks; sometimes he would snatch it up and twirl it round and round over his head, then bringing it down, with a bounce he would walk away backwards, shaking his fist at it. It would take him half the forenoon to clean two or three pairs of shoes, for each shoe as it was finished had to go through a course of shakings before Tom was satisfied it would sit firm. I used to like to look at him, and very often laughed at his pranks, but he didn't seem to care, for he never took any notice of my laughing. At first it amused my uncle and aunt, but they soon tired of it as he was of but little service to them, so my uncle sent him away, and got another whose name was Bradly, and he was worse than Tom Plant; for he was both lazy and stubborn; he would do only what he chose to do, and that was very little. A day or two after he came, my aunt's watch had run down, she went to the door and calling to Bradly, told him to go into the kitchen and look at the time-piece and tell her what o'clock it was. He answered, "Thank you, ma'am, I've been looking at the time-piece all day, and would rather not look at it any longer, thank you all the same." Aunty closed the door, and laughing, said to me, "I suppose the man does not know how to tell the time, and that ridiculous speech was made for an excuse." I thought I would soon find out whether he could or not. So the next morning I went into the kitchen and found Bradly sitting cozily by the fire, turning the spit, for my aunt had hung a piece of meat by the fire to roast, and had told him to keep the spit turned to prevent it burning. So I went up to him and said, "Please, Bradly, tell me what o'clock it is," he looked up at the time-piece and told me the exact time. Awhile after my aunt came in and said to him, "You must clean the knives and forks very nicely to-day, Bradly," he turned round quickly, saying, "Thank you, ma'am, I've been cleaning knives and forks all morning and would rather not clean any more to-day." Aunty said, "Why, Bradly, you are telling a story, you have not cleaned any knives and forks this morning, but you must clean them, for your master is going to bring company home to dinner." He answered, "Thank you all the same, ma'am, but I would rather not clean any more to-day." Nor did he, for my aunt could neither coax or scold him to clean them.

It was customary at that time to drink ale at the dinner table, and my uncle used to buy a small cask full at a time. One day he found the cask was empty, for he had neglected to have it replenished. So he took a pitcher and going to the door, called Bradly and said to him, "Go to Mr. Lipscomb's and get me a quart of the best ale," he replied, "Thank you, sir, I've been drinking ale all the morning, and would rather not drink any more to-day." My uncle said, "Why, my good man, if you have been drinking ale all the morning, I have had none, and I want you to go and get me some." He answered, "Thank you, all the same, sir, but I would rather not drink any more ale to-day." Aunty and I hearing the discussion, went to the door, there stood my uncle holding out the pitcher in one hand and the money in the other, and Bradly shaking his head, declaring he would rather not drink any more ale to-day. My aunt tried to make him understand what was wanted, but she failed to do so. At last my uncle got angry and told him if he did not be off he would break the pitcher over his head. They did not keep him long after that, for he was of no use whatever to them. Whether those two men obtained their discharge or not, I cannot say, for I never seen or heard anything of them after, but whenever I read or hear tell of persons who have committed any crime, shamming insanity for the purpose of evading the penalty of the law, it always reminds me of Tom Plant and Bradly.

SET DOWN THAT GLASS.

Set down that glass, taste not that wine,
　　Ere death o'ertakes you stop,
There's deadly poison in the cup,
　　Mingled with every drop.
Set down that glass and turn away,
　　Before it is too late,
Within its sparkling depth I see
　　The road to ruin's gate.

And down that road with rapid steps
　　Thousands are hurrying on,
Degraded and enslaved by rum,
　　Short is the race they run.
Brought to a level with the brute,
　　Mocked by the passer-by,
In shame and misery they live,
　　And oft in sin they die.

Oh, noble youth, with soul endowed,
Must this sad fate be thine,
Nay, rise, shake off the tyrant's chain,
And shun the sparkling wine.
Stand up and bruise the serpent's head,
Tis thine the power to do,
Forsake the road your feet have trod,
And virtue's path pursue.

Go not with those who seek strong drink,
Stand not in sinners' way,
And should the tempter thee assail,
For grace and wisdom pray
That God who marks the sparrows fall
Will hear the feeble prayer
Of him who cries in faith for help
To escape the tempter's snare.

THE SLAVE'S LAMENT.

(Composed after hearing a slave story read.)

They tore me from my native home.
    'Neath Afric's burning sky,
Where glad and free I used to roam,
    How happy then was I.

They bound me with a galling chain,
    I sank in dark despair,
I mourned, I pleaded, but in vain,
    No pitying eye was there.

They bore me from my native home,
    Across the ocean wave,
Here in a foreign land I roam,
    And toil—the white man's slave.

I met and loved my Nellie here,
    And she became my bride,
I spent one short and happy year
    With Nellie by my side.

One evening as the last bright ray
    Was fading in the west,
Poor Nellie passed from earth away,
    And sweetly sank to rest,

And I was left alone to bear
    My trials as before,
No one my grief and joy to share,
    I wished that life was o'er.

I long to lay me down to sleep,
    'Neath yonder willow tree,
Where flowers bright will wave and weep
    O'er Nellie dear and me.

MY GRANDFATHER.

I am now going to tell you about my dear, old grandfather, who long since passed away from earth to dwell in that beautiful world on high. A finer looking old gentleman you would not meet in a day's journey, and he was just as kind hearted as he was nice looking. He was loved and respected by all who knew him. For my part I thought him the very best grandfather in existence. I first remember seeing him seated in his large rocking chair reading, his spectacles resting quietly on his nose, looking as if they felt more at home there than in any other place, and I guess they did, it being but seldom they were anywhere else, for as grandpa was hard of hearing, he spent a great part of his time in reading. The few locks that remained around the lower part of his head were silvery white, the upper part being quite bald, but covered with a small, black velvet cap, which he always wore, as I suppose, to supply the want of the natural covering. Grandpa would never lie down to take a nap through the day, but would often fall asleep in his chair while reading. Sometimes the book or newspaper would drop from his hand; if it was a paper it would not be apt to wake him, but if a book the sound would immediately arouse him, and he would pick it up looking half sorry, half vexed, for he took great care of books, and did not like to see them made shabby by rough usage. I used to like to look at grandpa for he had a pleasing countenance, and when he spoke there was a tone of tenderness in his voice. He had a smile and kind word for all; his manner was gentle and affectionate, yet if opposed he was firm and self-willed; and it was not impossible for him to be put out of temper, but it was soon over, and the good natured look returned, making his face appear brighter than ever, like a summer sky after a storm. If I chanced to go into grandpa's room when he was about to shave, he would pretend not to see me until after he had put the lather on his face, preparatory to using the razor; then with a knowing twinkle in his eye, he would say, "Good morning, my dear, come and kiss me." Now, I always like to kiss grandpa, but this mode of procedure not only pleased me but highly amused me. So I would go to him and be very careful to kiss him fair and square on the lips, so as to avoid getting the soap suds in my own pretty little mouth, but which I did not always succeed in doing. This is what he called a barber's kiss. Grandpa was fond of music, and used to play very nicely on the flute. I also was fond of music, and loved to listen to the soft, rich tones of the instrument as they filled the room with sweet melody, while grandpa played the dear old tunes he once delighted to sing; for in his younger days he had been a good singer, but as he advanced in years his voice failed, so that when he would refresh his heart with music his flute was to him all in all.

I will now give a brief sketch of my grandfather's life. He was born on the 26th January, 1774, in the City of Bristol, England. While yet a child, death deprived him of his mother. As soon as old enough, he was placed at a boarding school, where he remained about ten or twelve years; when nineteen years of age he entered the British navy, and during the French war served three years on board His Majesty's ship *Caesar* (King George, the III., being then on the throne of England). It was on board of a man-of-war, and at the early age of twenty, he experienced a change of heart. An account of his conversion is given in his own words in a letter written to his father, of which the following is an extract; the original, though of distant date, is still preserved in the family:—

ON BOARD H.M. SHIP *CÆSAR*,

PLYMOUTH HARBOR, JANUARY 27TH, 1794.

MY DEAR PARENT,— Be not offended at my not writing before, but a particular reason withheld me which you shall know in my next, which I hope will shortly be. I hope, my dear father, you enjoy still a good state of health. I am (Glory to God) in health well, but in a spiritual state far from it.

I shall now open my mind to you. When first I came on board a man-of-war, I had some show of outward religion, but none of inward; my ears were saluted with torrents of oaths, execrations and curses and soon (with horror now I speak it) I was able to do the like myself. Though I was thus alienated from God, his watchful Providence still was over me. One day I saw a young man who appeared very melancholy. I asked him what was the matter. He would not tell me at first, but as I still urged him he at last told me he had been very wicked, and that frightful thoughts continually troubled him. This began to rouse me and my conscience, which was till now asleep, awakened, and I began to see what I was myself. I mentioned some texts of scripture, which had not till then come into my mind to him, which I also applied to myself. We now became constant companions. I found that this young man in a voyage to the East Indies, had been very intimate with a Roman Catholic, who had so far drawn him over to a good opinion of that persuasion as to kneel down on a Bible, and swear at the first port he made he would embrace that religion. I knew not how to advise him, but we were determined not to lead such a life as our former past had been, God being our helper. Our great Creator would not leave us, but sent us a gracious companion. About the middle of October we received a draft of men on board, in lieu of some that were sick and gone to the hospital, among whom was this man who had been pressed into the service at Dublin, but I knew him not till a month after. As I was walking the deck rather melancholy upon a Sunday, I saw him sitting reading a book which I thought to be a song book. I went and asked him if it was so, but to my great joy and surprise I found it to be Mr. Wesley's hymns; then I asked him if he was a Methodist, he made no answer, but turned to the title page, and there I saw his ticket pinned to it, by which I found he belonged to the society of Whitehaven, at which I could stay not longer, but flew to my former companion and told the joyful news. We returned together and spent that evening in such a manner as we had not since we had been in the ship.

Since that time we have been inseparable companions, and we have found him very beneficial to us. He has a small but valuable library, containing a Bible, one volume of Mr. Wesley's sermons, a hymn book and an explanation of some chapters in Ezekiel. In the reading of these we spend most part of our leisure time. Oh! my dear father, pray for me, for I now see what a state I am in. Oh! may the blessed God give me more and more, not only to see but to feel and sorrow for the lost state I am in; but praised be his name, I am not now without hope, but that ere long I shall be enabled (through the blood of the ever blessed Jesus) to rejoice in a sense of His pardoning love. These scriptures give great comfort to me. "Surely the Lord's hand is not shortened that he cannot love." "Whoever cometh to me I will in no wise cast out." "Never saw I the righteous forsaken or his seed begging their bread."

LETTER.

Written by my Grandfather to his Father, when about to sail in defence of his country.

ST. HELLEN'S ROADS,

ON BOARD H.M. SHIP *CAESAR*,

April 18th, 1794

HONORED FATHER,— What an unspeakable blessing it is that God has bestowed upon us that, though we at a great distance separated, yet are enabled as it were to converse together.

An opportunity offering, I have embraced it, sincerely hoping it may find you in perfect health, as this through the blessing of God leaves me. I should have sent you a letter by Mrs. Williams, but we were unexpectedly ordered to sea. We accordingly sailed the next morning. We are now in company with Lord Howe's fleet, lying at St. Hellen's waiting for a wind; we have made two fruitless attempts to go out.

How eagerly do I wish, my father, that peace may be established again on our Isle. How wretched is a life on board a man-of-war, where nothing is heard but the language of hell.

Oh! may the devouring sword cease, and the thundering cannon be heard no more, that I may once more fly to the arms, that under God, was the protection of my infant days. How cautious would I be again to leave them; but though my present situation is so unhappy, yet I will not repine at the providence of God, who has placed me in it, but patiently wait the Lord's pleasure.

We are now about to sail in defence of our country, and in it perhaps I shall fall a sacrifice, but should this be my lot I will strive to meet it with fortitude and resignation, trusting in Him alone who is the disposer of all events. But ere I conclude I must bid you farewell for the present, hoping again to see you; but should the case be otherwise, farewell forever, and should we never meet on earth, oh! may we meet in heaven, where the wicked cease from troubling, and the weary be at rest. May this be the happy lot where I shall pay nature debt of

YOUR AFFECTIONATE AND DUTIFUL SON.

While on board a man-of-war my grandfather was in several engagements, one battle in particular he always spoke of with much pride. It was fought on the 1st day of June, 1794, and known as Lord Howe's glorious victory, an account of which is given by my grandfather in a letter written to his father two days after the battle, of which the following is a copy:—

H.M. SHIP CÆSAR, June 3rd, 1794.

HONORED FATHER,— Assist me to praise and glorify Almighty God, for the wonderful protection He has vouchsafed to bestow on me, unworthy as I am. We left St. Hellen's on May the 2nd, but I shall not recount the whole of our cruise. Suffice it to say that May the 28th, we fell in with the French fleet. They being to windward we could not bring them to action till 8 o'clock at night, and then only a few ships engaged. The 29th we formed the line twenty-five ships in each, and our ship leading the van. But we being so far to leeward, only eleven ships came up, who engaged the whole of the French line, our ship engaged one of her own force for two hours. We afterwards passed the whole of the enemy's line, receiving the fire of every ship in order to bring the rest of our ships in action, which we did, and broke the enemy's line and drove them to leeward. At about six in the evening the two fleets separated, the action having lasted about seven or eight hours. We had two men killed and thirteen wounded, but heaven preserved me. We did not see our enemies again till Saturday, the 30th, at 2 o'clock in the afternoon, by reason of a thick fog during the interval. We came up with them about 8 o'clock at night, but did not come to action till Sunday, June the 1st; about nine o'clock we began and about twelve it ended. We sunk two line of battle ships in action, dismasted ten, and eight of them we took prisoners. Six are now on their passage with us to England, and two more sunk since the action. We had about ten killed and thirty wounded. But thanks be to God who gave us the victory, I am still alive and unhurt. This is a short but faithful account. Our shipping being sadly shattered, and our Admiral wishing the glorious news should reach England sooner than we could bring it, has dispatched a frigate; by her I found means to send this letter, which I hope will find you in good health. Please excuse the writing, things not being at sea as it is on shore, and I having so short a notice. My next shall be more precise.

I remain,

YOUR DUTIFUL AND AFFECTIONATE SON.

My grandfather lived to be eighty-four years of age, but he never forgot the glorious 1st of June. In 1796 he left the navy, and in 1797 was married at Plymouth, a town in the west of England, where he resided for many years, carrying on the business of a wine merchant. In 1822 he, with his wife and their five youngest children, came to America, landing at St. Andrew's, New Brunswick, where he immediately obtained a situation as teacher of a grammar school. He had been in America but six years, when he was called to mourn the loss of his beloved wife. He never married again, though some of his children were quite young when their mother died, giving as a reason his wish to train his children himself, which he did, and in after years had the satisfaction of seeing them become professing Christians and worthy members of society.

In 1849 he received a silver medal, sent him by the Queen, he being then 75 years of age, and one of the only two of Her Majesty's subjects then known to be living, who was in the battle of the 1st of June. In 1857 he, with one son and two daughters and their families, left New Brunswick, and came to Ontario. His youngest daughter, with whom he had always resided, settled in Colchester, where, in 1858, after a short illness, my grandfather died and was buried. His end was peace.

CONTENTION BETWEEN THE LIFE AND DEATH ANGEL.

LIFE ANGEL.

Oh, thou with ebon wings and icy hands,
Spare this dear object of fond parent's love,
Break not the silver chord of life so soon,
Haste not from earth this spirit to remove;
Go to some aged one, weary of earth,
Who waits with longing heart to welcome thee,
Who fain would quit the feeble, wasting frame;
Go thou and set that captive spirit free.

DEATH ANGEL.

Nay! speak not thus, do thou not know that I
Am sent by One who is too wise to err;
Too kind to be unjust, in mercy now
He bids me end this spirit's sojourn here.
And now behold! this spirit I release,
That it may mount to realms of endless day,
E'er earth's alluring charms entice the soul
From virtue's path and wisdom's pleasant way.

LIFE ANGEL.

Oh, spare this one so fondly cherished here,
Why must thou pluck this tender bud so soon,
Ere it unfolds in youth's fair opening spring,
Ere it's rare worth and loveliness are known.
Why must this one thus early pass away?
Why one so young be numbered with the dead?
Withhold thy hand till age has dimmed these eyes,
And from those cheeks the bloom of youth has fled.

DEATH ANGEL.

I cannot pass her by, now is the time,
Ere sin and folly doth ensnare the soul;
Ere she hath trod the path to hoary age,
Angels may weep that she from grace did fall.
And now behold! I pluck this tender bud,

And angel spirits wait to bear it hence,
To a celestial bower, where it may bloom
In beauty there and holy innocence.

LIFE ANGEL.

Oh, let her tarry yet awhile on earth,
A guardian angel will her steps attend,
To shield her from the subtle tempter's snare,
And guard and guide her safely to the end;
Oh, stay thy hand, hush not this prattling voice,
Take her not from a mother's fond embrace,
Oh, let the rose of health return again,
No other on this earth can fill her place.

DEATH ANGEL.

Nay, He who gave this gentle creature being,
Now kindly takes her from the ills to come,
And shining ones around her bed do wait,
To waft the spirit to its heavenly home;
On earth a guardian angel hath not power,
To keep the soul secure from every sin.
Life is a battle with a deadly foe,
And many fight, but few there be that win.

LIFE ANGEL.

Oh, must this form low in the dust be laid,
This heart no more to taste the joys of earth,
Must this fair brow be shaded by the grave,
No more to wear the smiles of childish mirth;
Behold those mourners who surround her couch,
Their eyes suffused with tears of heartfelt grief,
Oh, wilt thou break the tender ties of love,
And of their darling those fond hearts bereave.

DEATH ANGEL.

Their mourning will endure but for awhile,
The parting scenes of earth will soon be o'er,
Ere long I shall be sent to summon them,
To meet again where partings are no more;
Then in that land where saints and angels dwell,

This one they loved so dearly here below
Will, at the portal of that blest abode
Welcome each one as from this world they go.

LIFE ANGEL.

Oh, must thou then remove this dear one now,
Oh, must the feeble pulse now cease to beat,
And must thou take her to thy cold embrace,
And bear her to the tomb, thy dark retreat;
Oh, must I now resign my precious charge,
Relentless one, in vain I plead with thee,
Already now I feel thy chilling breath,
And from thy awful presence I must flee.

DEATH ANGEL.

What though this form must moulder in the tomb?
The happy soul shall upwards wing its way,
To dwell forever in a world of bliss,
Where all is fair, and nothing can decay;
I must fulfil my mission on the earth,
I but obey the master's mandate now,
He gently calls the spirit I release,
And sets my seal upon this infant brow.

LUKE ANSON.

IN TWO CHAPTERS.

CHAPTER I.

MISPLACED CONFIDENCE.

Mr. Vane was an old gentleman, who for many years had been confined to his room, and at times was unable even to rise from his bed without assistance. He had a comfortable home and money more than sufficient to support him in easy independence the remainder of his days. But the old man must have often felt very lonely, for he had no relatives that any of his neighbors knew of, his wife having died before reaching middle age, and he had no children to cheer and comfort him in his declining years. His home was kept in order and he was waited on by a hired housekeeper, a kind, quiet, elderly woman. Mr. Vane, after first becoming unable to leave his room, had engaged a barber at a stated salary to come to his house every morning, for the purpose of shaving and washing him, and assist in arranging his toilet for the day.

One morning about the time our story begins, his barber informed him that he intended leaving the town, and recommended to his service a young man named Anson, who, if Mr. Vane was willing, he would send to him the next morning.

Mr. Vane consented, at the same time expressing his regret at having to part with his old friend, for as he said he had become accustomed to his ways, and he would miss him very much. The other consoled the old gentleman by telling him he had no doubt but that he would soon learn to like young Anson quite as well, as he knew him to be a very nice young man. Mr. Vane said he hoped it would be so and the two friends parted. The next morning Luke Anson rapped at the door of Mr. Vane's house and was admitted by the housekeeper, who showed him to the room where he found Mr. Vane, who received him kindly, and after arranging matters to the satisfaction of both parties, Luke immediately entered upon his duty, and by the time he had completed his morning task Mr. Vane had formed an opinion quite in favor of the young man, an opinion which further acquaintance served only to strengthen. Luke was a person of prepossessing appearance, easy and agreeable in manner, with a frank open countenance; and as time passed Mr. Vane became more and more attached to him, and now looked forward to his coming with pleasure, especially when he had promised to bring something to read that he knew would interest him. Now and then, Mr. Vane would invite him to spend an hour or two with him on a Sunday afternoon, and sometimes of an evening, Luke would call in to have a chat with his old friend. Thus matters stood, when one evening, as Luke was about to wish him good night, Mr. Vane took from beneath his pillow a key, and handing it to Luke, told him to go to the bureau which stood in one corner of the room and bring him a box which he would find in the top drawer. Luke did as he was desired, and placed the box on a stand near the bed. Mr. Vane raised the lid of the box, took out a large leather purse, and unclasping it poured the contents out on the bed. It was gold. "This is mine," he said to Luke, as he stirred the glittering heap with his fingers, "all my own, but I shall not live long enough to need but little of it. You have been very kind to me and if you continue so, when I die I will leave the greater part of this gold to you; the rest I must give to my housekeeper, who has also shown me great kindness."

Luke thanked Mr. Vane, saying that what he had done more than was his duty had only been a pleasure for him to do, and was not deserving so great a reward.

"Yes, yes, it shall be as I say," said Mr. Vane, "it shall be as I say." He then gathered up the shining coin, put them back in the purse, and clasping it laid it in the box, closed the lid, and requested Luke to put it where he had found it, who did so, and after locking the drawer returned the key to Mr. Vane and bade him good night. After this Mr. Vane would often ask Luke to bring his money and count it for him, and as often did he repeat his promise to leave the greater part of his gold to him. Little did he think of the great temptation he was laying in the path of that young man. Little did he know what would be the result of his misplaced confidence.

CHAPTER II.

THE CRIME DISCOVERED AND CONFESSED.

One fine morning in summer, the neighbors noticed that Mr. Vane's house remained closed unusually late, but no one thought much about it until, as the day advanced and there was no sign of life in or about the house, they began to wonder what could be the matter, but nothing serious was suspected, and night closed in without the cause being discovered. The next morning, as soon as the people were astir, all eyes were turned in the direction of Mr. Vane's house, but not a door or window was open to let in the pure air and the warm sunlight. By noon quite a number of people were collected in front of the house, for the authorities of the town had been informed of the circumstance and detectives sent to make an investigation, and, who had just made their appearance on the spot. One of them mounted the steps and knocked loudly at the door, but received no answer. After repeated knockings and no response, the door was forced open and what a ghastly sight was there. On the floor lay the body of the poor, old housekeeper; near her lay a brass candlestick covered with blood, evidently the weapon with which she had been murdered. The walls and floor were also spattered with blood. After giving orders for the body to be attended to, the detectives passed upstairs and into the room of Mr. Vane—the walls and floor of which were also spattered with blood. On the bed lay the corpse of the old man. On the floor lay a lath-hammer covered with blood, plainly

showing it to be the instrument used in taking the life
of Mr. Vane. Both bodies were carefully attended to,
and a coroner's inquest held. Their verdict was, that
those two inoffensive old people had come to their
death by being cruelly murdered by some person or
persons unknown.

For some weeks this dark deed remained shrouded
in mystery, but at last suspicion fell on young Anson,
who had suddenly and unaccountably become flush
of money. He was therefore arrested, as was also his
father, who was suspected of being an accomplice to
his son's guilt. When charged of the crime, both father
and son pleaded innocent, but when brought before
the bar of justice and tried, they were found guilty. A
young man who had been an intimate acquaintance
of young Anson, gave his evidence as follows:—"I was
at the home of Anson on the evening of the murder.
About eight o'clock young Anson went out, saying he
would go and bring some oranges.

He was gone a long time, it being after nine o'clock
when he returned. When he came in he appeared much
agitated. His hands, face and clothing were covered
with blood. He said that he had met some ruffians who
laid hands on him, and that he had had a hard struggle
with them, barely escaping with his life. His mother
told him he had better go and wash, and change his
clothes. He then went upstairs, followed by his father.
Immediately on entering his room I distinctly heard a
sound as if a large quantity of money had been thrown
on the bed, but I didn't think anything of it at the time.
In about half an hour young Anson came down again,

looking very pale. I then left the house."

Other witnesses were called and examined, and the testimony of all went to prove the guilt of both father and son, who claimed they were innocent even after the sentence of death had been pronounced on one, and banishment for life on the other. They were then remanded to jail—the younger Anson to remain there till the day of his execution, and the elder Anson to stay there until brought forth to be placed on board the ship which was to bear him from home and friends forever.

About twelve o'clock one night, while in prison, the elder Anson was aroused by a slight noise in his cell, and looking up he saw a tall figure clothed in white, who said to him in a sepulchral tone of voice, "Anson, Anson, tell the truth," and after pronouncing these words, slowly and solemnly the figure noiselessly withdrew. In the morning Anson desired that a minister might be sent for, saying that his mind had been so troubled during the night that he wished to confess without further delay. As soon as the minister arrived, Anson, pale and trembling, told the whole truth.

I will not harrow the feelings of my readers with the horrible details of his confession. Suffice it to say, that though he himself had no hand in murdering Mr. Vane and his housekeeper, yet he was fully aware of his son's intentions to commit the crime, in order to gain possession of the money he knew to be in Mr. Vane's house. After the dreadful deed was done and the gold obtained, and fearing to keep it in the house, the father and son together went and buried it. "And now," said he in conclusion, "if you will take me where I shall direct you I will show you where the money is hidden." A cab was then brought, and Anson, handcuffed and closely guarded was placed in it and driven off in the direction pointed out by him. The way led them some distance beyond the limits of the town through a thick wood. On arriving at an opening by the road side, at a word from Anson the cab was stopped and the prisoner and guards alighted and entered the opening. Anson then pointed out a large tree, at the foot of which, after removing the sod and an inch or two of earth, the box containing Mr. Vane's purse of gold was discovered and taken charge of. They then re-entered the cab, drove back to town, and Anson was returned to his cell.

The spirit he supposed he had seen was no other than the turnkey of the jail who had adopted this plan to draw him into a confession, and which, is already known, proved a success. Not many days after his confession Anson, with a number of other convicts, left his native country for Van Diemen's Land, but before the ship had reached her destination he fell sick and died, and was buried in the sea.

The younger Anson, who maintained a sullen silence to the last, at the appointed time suffered the penalty of the law. Thus, in shame and misery, ended those two lives. "What does it profit a man if he gains the whole world, and loses his own soul."

BLIGHTED FLOWERS.

See the last fair flowers of summer,
    Blighted by the autumn blast,
Faintly now their fragrance raiseth,
    As an infant breathes its last.
See the faded leaves now scattered,
    On the ground they scentless lay,
Leaves that filled the air with perfume
    On the last bright summer day.

Then the gentle breezes sighing,
    Bore their fragrance through the vale,
Each and every radiant blossom
    Lends its odour to the gales.
All their bright and gorgeous colours,
    Then appeared so fresh and gay,
But their beauty has departed
    Since the last bright summer day.

Frost has nipped the fairest flowers,
    Autumn winds have laid them low,
Tender buds not yet unfolded
    Perish ere their worth we know.
None escape the ruthless tempest,
    As it hurries on its way.
Blighting by its breath the blossoms
    Of the last bright summer day.

SWEET CONTENT.

ON HEARING A POOR MAN SINGING AT HIS WORK.

I am poor, yet I am cheerful,
  Happy as the bird that sings;
Never sad, nor never fearful,
  Sweet content each moment brings.

I am poor, yet life is pleasant,
  Humble though my lot may be;
Sweet content is ever present,
  Making earth a heaven to me.

I am poor, yet I am healthy,
  This is all the boon I crave;
I never envy those who are wealthy,
  While my health and strength I have.

I am poor, yet I will never
  Sigh for earthly treasures vain,
Sweet content smiles on me ever,
  Never will my heart complain.

I am poor, yet by my labor,
  Food and raiment are supplied;
I, less worthy than my neighbor,
  Must not boast nor speak with pride.

I am poor, yet without number
  Heaven's blessings rest on me;
Labor brings refreshing slumber,
  I'm contented, glad and free.

THE EVENING BREEZE.

Soft sighs the gentle breezes
　From the distant hills,
Sweet is the breath of evening,
　Through the vale it steals,
On through the smiling meadows,
　Whispering in the trees,
Rich with the breath of roses,
　Comes the evening breeze.

How like a laughing fairy
　Doth the zephyr play,
Kissing sweet buds and blossoms,
　Fragrant and gay.
Onwards it steals but softly,
　Sighing in the trees,
Low is the gentle murmur,
　Of the evening breeze.

A CONVERSION IN A BARBER SHOP.

The following story was once told me by my mother, which I will give in her own words:—

One fine summer morning, a long time ago, I was walking very leisurely through Newcastle market. As I was sauntering along I observed a lady walking a little ahead of me, whom I knew must be an old and highly esteemed friend of mine, for although I had not seen her for ten years I recognized her figure; so quickening my steps I was soon by her side and said, "Good morning, Mrs. Smith." She turned towards me and replied, "Good morning, Miss. You have the advantage of me, I do not know you." I asked her if she did not recollect the little girl who was staying with her whilst she lived at Portsmouth. She said, "Yes, I do, but it cannot be possible that you are her." I said I am the same. She expressed much joy at our meeting so unexpectedly, and said you must go home with me, for Mr. Smith would be exceedingly glad to see you. As we were walking along she asked me if I had come to Newcastle on business. I told her no, I was married, and my husband was mate of a ship then lying at one of the docks.

We soon reached the house, and Mr. Smith was indeed glad to see his little girl, as he called me, and laughed heartily at the idea as he said of my being a 'married woman.' As I knew my husband could not leave his ship till the evening I remained with them all day.

In the afternoon Mr. Smith went out to take a walk. Soon after he was gone Mrs. Smith asked me if I had not observed a change in Mr. Smith's manner. I answered I had, a very great change for the better. She said, "Yes, he is a good Christian man now. I will tell you about his conversion." She asked me if I did not remember what a profane man he was, and how grieved she used to be at hearing him swear so badly? I told her I did, and how earnestly she prayed for his conversion. She said, "Yes, I did, and I knew then that my Heavenly Father heard my prayers and would answer them in His own good time." She then said, "When we came to Newcastle to live and had settled down, in a quiet way, I joined the Methodist Church. At first I used to ask Mr. Smith to go to church with me, but he always refused, making some frivolous excuse. One morning he went out to go to the barber shop to get shaved. When he came home again he sat down by the fire, and leaning his elbow on his knee, held his handkerchief up to his face, and I knew he was crying. Such an unusual occurrence alarmed me, so I went to him and asked him to tell me what had happened. He rose from his seat and said, "Dorothy, dear, I know you have prayed for my conversion these many years and your prayers have been answered this morning. When I got to the barber shop there was no one in but the young apprentice. As I never let any one shave me but the master, I asked him how long it would be before his master returned, and he said he did not expect him in till the afternoon, but, he added, 'I can shave you, sir.' Now, as he knew I never let him shave me it riled my temper, and I began cursing and swearing and calling him very bad names. In the midst of it all the poor boy fell on his knees by the barber's chair and offered up a fervent prayer for me—oh, so fervent that it touched my heart—and I, too, fell on my knees by the side of the chair and told him to keep on praying until his prayers were answered, and he did. He cried and prayed, and I cried and groaned. At length the string of my tongue was loosed, and I, too, could pray, and we both prayed together. This poor lad fairly shouted with joy when he heard me praying. In a little while we arose from our knees, and after shaking hands I left him standing there blessing and praising God for so great a salvation."

Mrs. Smith was silent, and we wiped the tears from our eyes. After a few minutes she said to me, "My dear, young friend, I have not words to express the joy I experienced that morn," but, she added,

"I thought what must be the rejoicing among the angels." She then said it happened on a Thursday, and in the evening there was a service in the church that I attended. I did not have to ask Mr. Smith to go with me for he was ready and waiting long before I was. He paid great attention to the sermon, and has ever since been a consistent member of the Methodist church, and he has never let anyone shave him but the young apprentice.

LEARNING TO DIVE.

A STORY FOR BOYS.

Johnny Edwards, though but fourteen years of age, was a good swimmer, and was anxiously trying to learn to dive, but he found it a more difficult task than he at first imagined it would be, for with all his practice he did not seem to improve. He would swim out into deep water and make a plunge downwards with all his might, but the instant he touched bottom he would rise again to the surface, just as a rubber ball bounces up when thrown down with force. One day Johnny went alone to have a swim, and after spending some time in fruitless attempts at diving, a bright thought came into his mind, and hastily swimming to the shore, he looked around until he had found two stones of equal size, and taking one in each hand, marched off to a steep bank several feet above the water. Now, said he, those stones will take me down, and after I have counted fifteen, I will let go of them and come up again. So saying he sprang into the water and down he went. On arriving at the bottom he began to count one, two, three. It was hard work to keep from breathing, and he was beginning to feel queer, but he would try and hold out to the end. Four, five, the water rushed into his mouth and nostrils, and he knew no more until he found himself wrapped in a coat, and lying on the bank with a man kneeling beside him, doing all he could to restore him to consciousness. "Where am I," asked Johnny as soon as he could speak. "You are all right, now, I guess," said the man, "but if you had stayed down there awhile longer, you would never have seen daylight again." "But how did you know I was down there," asked Johnny, who saw by the man's wet clothes that it was he who had saved him from drowning. "I saw you spring into the water with those stones in your hands, but had not time to warn you of the danger, for I knew if you were left alone you would not come up again alive, so I ran as quickly as I could and taking off my hat and coat, plunged into the water, dived down, and brought you up in time to save your life."

"And now," said the man, "let me warn you never to take stones or anything that is heavy in your hands when you are going into the water." Johnny, who by this time had so far recovered as to be able to walk, said he thought he would be apt to remember the warning. The man then accompanied him home, and after receiving the thanks of Johnny and his friends, bade him good bye. Johnny gave up learning to dive, but he never forgot that day's adventure.

TO THE MEMORY OF LITTLE ROSA.

The following lines were composed for a family of eight children, on the death of their little sister, a sweet child of two and a half years, whose delicate constitution and rare beauty made her the pet of the household:—

The angels came and bore away
    One of our little band;
We know our little sister lives
    Up in the better land.
Her little body we have laid
    Down in the silent grave,
And when another spring shall come,
    Sweet flowers will o'er her wave.

Oh! how we loved her when on earth
    She used to live with us,
Fair as the lilies, spotless bell,
    Our little Rosay was,
And now we think of her above,
    Among the cherubs there,
More beautiful than when on earth—
    An angel bright and fair.

She has a little harp of gold,
    And wears a robe of white,
She sings the song that angels know,
    And dwells in glory bright.
She never will be sick again,
    Nor suffer any more,
She's safe in the good Shepherd's fold
    From every ill secure.

We have a brother and sister there,
    Who with the angels roam,
Perhaps they were with those who came,
    To take our Rosay home.
Now those three cherubs hand in hand,
    Wander amidst the flowers,
That bloom in that bright world above,
    In the celestial bowers.

We would not call her back to earth,
    She is so happy there;
But when we fondly think of her,
    There falls the silent tear,
She has escaped the sin and snares
    Of earth's alluring charms,
And now our little Rosay rests
    In the good Shepherd's arms.

She never will return to us,
    But we may go to her,
And there no parting tears shall fall,
    Death cannot enter there.
Then let us all prepare to meet
    Her in that world above,
Where saints and angels all unite
    To sing redeeming love.

ANNIE BOWDEN.

The last words of the marriage ceremony were pronounced and Albert Blake and Annie Bowden were man and wife, and would have been as happy as any other new married couple if Albert had not to go away so soon and for so long a time. It happened thus. Albert had come to the town of B a stranger seeking employment, and not caring where he went, had several weeks previous to his marriage taken a situation as captain's steward on board of a man-of-war then preparing for a three years' cruise and would now be ready to sail in one month. Since his acquaintance and engagement with Annie he had several times expressed a wish that he had not joined the ship, but always ended by saying as if thinking aloud, "It is just as well, I suppose, just as well."

That month passed quickly and pleasantly away,

and when the day arrived on which the ship was to sail Annie bade her husband good-bye with a sad heart, and standing on the pier watched the ship sail away with tear-dimmed eyes. Poor Annie; could she have seen the dark cloud which was even then rising in her sky and which would so soon burst in a storm of sorrow on her head, she would have been tempted to have plunged into the deep blue water and hidden herself from its fury in the cold bosom of the ocean. But a kind Providence has wisely veiled the future from mortal sight, and with a sense of loneliness she had never before known Annie walked slowly back to her father's house, for it had been arranged that she should remain with her parents until her husband's return.

One morning, about three months after her husband's departure, as she lay on the bed resting after a long walk, her mother came into the room and told her there was a strange lady down stairs in the parlor who wished to see her. Annie arose, and wondering who the lady could be and what her business was with her, went down stairs, followed by her mother. As soon as she entered the room the lady arose, and advancing towards her said, "Is this Mrs. Albert Blake?" Annie bowing, replied, "Yes." Then, said the lady, "I am sorry for you; Heaven help you to bear what I have to tell you. Albert Blake was a married man, and I am his wife." Annie heard the last words as if in a dream and staggering back, fell fainting in the arms of her mother, who, assisted by the lady, laid her on the sofa. Some time elapsed before she could be restored to consciousness, and when she at last opened her eyes their brightness was all gone, and in them there was a look of hopeless despair. For a long while she did not move or speak but seemed as if stunned by the blow. Could she have wept it would have been well for her, but no tears came to her relief; and it was weeks before she recovered from the fit of illness into which the terrible shock had thrown her. When her father heard the news his rage knew no bounds; he immediately wrote to Blake, informing him that his villainy had been discovered, and threatening to shoot him if he ever made his appearance again in that town.

Blake, however, died in the East Indies shortly after receiving the letter. Before dying he wrote to Annie, confessing the whole truth, and by way of excusing himself told the following story:—"When nineteen years of age I was forced into a marriage with Harriet Lee by my own and her parents to gratify a wish long cherished by them, they being old and intimate friends, and each possessing a small fortune. Their object in bringing about a marriage between their only children, Harriet and myself, was to unite their fortunes. And so, though much against my will, we were married—for I never did nor I never could like Harriet, her cold nature and overbearing manner repelled me—and after dragging through five years of miserable existence I left her, but with the intention of not marrying again so long as I knew she was living. Nor should I have done so had I not met and loved you." Annie read the letter, of which the foregoing is an extract, with feelings that cannot be described, but after a fit of passionate weeping she grew more calm, and as time wore on became more reconciled to her fate, but never regained her happy spirits and blithe manner. The sparkle never returned to her eye nor the rose to her cheek. She never spoke of her sorrow, but an expression of settled sadness on her pale face told how great had been the mental suffering she had endured.

THE SONG OF THE INDIAN.

When brightly shines the rising sun,
    To chase away the morning dew;
With cheerful heart and merry song,
    I push from shore my light canoe.

When soft winds gently steal along,
    O'er rippling waters deep and blue;
Then loud I sing my morning song,
    As swiftly glides my light canoe.

The white man's wealth I envy not,
    For stately halls and honor too,
I'd never exchange my humble lot,
    I'm happy in my light canoe.

The white men love their glittering gold,
    Their gallant ships they proudly view;
I'd rather roam thus free and bold,
    And gladly own my light canoe.

From early dawn till close of day,
    I wander on the ocean blue;
Till twilight gathers o'er my way,
    Then homeward glides my light canoe.

THE BIRDS.

I often think the birds are part of creation that did not come under the curse in the fall of man. They always seem to be a little bit of paradise left to remind us of what a happy lot ours would have been had not sin robbed us of innocence and sweet peace of mind. The birds enjoy life as no other creatures do. Insects are always either hard at work or hurrying aimlessly from one place to another. The beasts are ever eagerly searching for food, and are satisfied only when they are eating. Even man is prone to wander, and how often is the mind disturbed by fretting, doubting and fearing.

It would be well if we could lay to heart the lesson taught us by the birds. They receive and enjoy present blessings with apparent gratitude and trust heaven for the future. The result is they alone are really happy.

Their little hearts seem always full of gladness; they sing alike when the sun is shining and when the rain is falling; in the morning they warble out their hymns of praise, and in the evening they fill the air with sweet melody.—Yea, all day long they wing their flight from tree to tree, or rest in the cool shade of the leafy branches. Their happy twitter and merry song may be heard even when darkness veils the earth; they are not all silent ever and anon; the pensive song of the night bird falls on the ear, cheering the belated and way worn traveller like the sweet notes of a silver bell. Who can walk through the woods on a fine summer morning and listen to the thousand and one voices of the feathered songsters, without the heart being stirred with feelings of gratitude to Him who taught the dear birds to sing, and though there are so many, yet not a discordant sound or feeble strain is heard. All join heart and voice in a full and complete chorus.

LINES ON THE DEATH OF A FRIEND.

A dear loved one has been removed
From earth's encumbering care;
The Saviour beckoned her away,
Eternal joys to share.
Her gentle spirit took its flight
On angel pinions borne;
Up to the world of endless bliss,
And heaven's eternal morn.

Ere she had gained the shining shore,
The pearly gates appeared;
And when cold Jordan's stream was crossed,
The heavenly armies cheered.
Yes, then the heavenly arches rang,
With one triumphant song;
As her bright spirit entered in,
And joined the glorious throng.

Her angel form is now arrayed
In robes of spotless white;
The victor's crown and palm are hers,
And endless glory bright.
Sickness no more can waste her frame,
Death cannot enter there;
Her spirit rests in sweet release,
From sorrow sin and care.

And would we call her from that land,
Of such exquisite bliss;
And wish her to return again,
To such a world as this?
Nay, blessed are the dead who die
With all their sins forgiven;
And from this vale of tears arise
To join the host of heaven.

Yea, mourning ones, no longer weep,
  For her you fondly loved;
But a short time she's gone before,
  And waits for you above.
Think not upon the mouldering dust
  That lies in yonder tomb;
Her spirit is not there, but past
  Beyond it chilling gloom.

Prepare to meet her in that land,
  Where all is bright and fair;
That when the toils of life are o'er,
  You may her gladness share.
Life is but short—a troubled dream,
  Our days are as the grass;
But heavenly joys can never fade,
  They will forever last.

THE CHILD'S PRAYER.

On hearing of a little girl who, one stormy night after saying her evening prayers, added a few words asking God to take care of the sailors, then with firm faith that her prayer was heard and would be answered, she laid her head on the pillow and fell into a sweet and peaceful sleep.

'Twas on a dark and dreary night,
    When stormy winds blew fierce and loud;
Ere resting on her downy bed,
    A little maiden form was bowed.
Her soft sweet voice in prayer arose,
    For wanderers on the mighty deep;
With tearful eyes she pleads to God,
    The sailor's life to safely keep.

Oh, God, I hear the tempest roar,
    In faith I do draw near to Thee;
Oh, please take care of those who now
    Are out upon the stormy sea.
I know that Thou alone can save,
    For fearful is the night and dark;
Oh let one little star appear,
    To guide the frail and tossing bark.

Her prayer arose on wings of faith,
    And now the gentle maiden slept;
The storm still raged in fury wild,
    As o'er the land and sea it swept
But who can tell what that sweet prayer
    And childlike faith had done to save
Some wanderer on the ocean wide,
    From sinking in a watery grave.

That prayer for one bright little star,
    Perchance was answered from above;
And to the sailor's heart it proved
    A messenger of hope and love.
And guided by its feeble ray,
    Some safe retreat the wanderer found;
Until the angry storm had ceased,
    And morning shed its glory round.

THE SCOFFER CONVERTED.

"There is a young lady going to preach in the Ranter's church this evening," said James Turner to his two companions, "let us go and have a little sport at her expense." "Agreed," said they, and away they went. On arriving at the church, notwithstanding the service had already begun, they with no little noise entered, took a seat near the door, and commenced talking in loud whispers to the great annoyance of the congregation, but when the second hymn was concluded, and Miss Harding, the young lady who was to preach, arose, and in a clear firm voice gave out the text and began her discourse, the attention of everyone was arrested. Even the three young men near the door ceased their whispering, and all listened attentively as the speaker proceeded. She grew more and more earnest and eloquent, solemnly warning sinners of their danger and kindly inviting them to the Saviour assuring them of peace and pardon through faith in Him. At the close of the sermon an invitation was extended to those who felt themselves sinners, and wished to be saved to come forward, and among the first to kneel at the penitent seat was James Turner. The arrow of conviction had pierced his heart, and he rested not until he found peace in believing.

From that time he regularly attended the meetings and eventually became a member of the church, nor was this all; after once seeing and speaking with Miss Harding, he could not forget the pleasing countenance and engaging manner of that young lady, and so it came to pass that in just five weeks from the evening on which he went to make sport of her preaching, she became his wife. His parents, who were wealthy people of the world, at first objected to their only son marrying a poor, religious fanatic as they termed Miss Harding, but on further acquaintance with her they changed their minds, and were quite reconciled to the union, the result of which was that she, under God was the means of bringing the whole family into the fold of the good Shepherd.

THE BLESSINGS OF THE SABBATH.

After a week of work and worry, as Saturday evening draws near, with what a sense of thankfulness do we realize that the Sabbath is at hand. This day's duty done then for awhile the tired brain and limbs may rest, the busy mind cease planning, and a soul refreshing season may be enjoyed by those who are interested in their eternal welfare. Oh! what a blessing that one day in seven is set aside on which we may shake off the many worldly cares that have clustered around the heart during the past week, and turn the thoughts heavenward to where a sweeter and more lasting rest awaits all those who hold out to the end of the Christian journey. As the weary traveller stops to rest under a tree by the road side, and is refreshed by eating the fruit from its branches and drinking from the clear spring that bursts from the ground at his feet, then with strength and courage renewed, goes on his way prepared to surmount all the difficulties that may lay in his path; so a Sabbath well spent prepares us the more easily to overcome all the trials and temptations of the ensuing week, and while we refrain as far as possible from all that is of a worldly nature, and strive to be like the beloved disciple John, in the spirit on the Lord's day, we cannot fail to be benefitted both temporally and spiritually. God in tender mercy and loving kindness gave us the Sabbath on which to rest and meditate. Not only the rich, but even the very poorest may avail themselves of the privileges, and enjoy the blessings of the day, but oh! how many there are who, instead of improving the time, waste the precious hours in idleness or in pleasure seeking, and by so doing disobey the command of God, and treat his kindness with ingratitude. For without the Sabbath life would be a perpetual round of toil, a dreary waste, a continual drudgery, and the hours of rest so limited that it would be next to impossible for man to attend to the welfare of his immortal soul. But with that blessed day comes rest for the body, and the influence of all that is good and pure to the mind.

Again, without the Sabbath life would be robbed of much that is bright and beautiful. For on a fine Sunday morning in summer does not all nature seem to rejoice; the flowers appear more fair, the birds sing sweeter, the children are less boisterous, the parents less impatient, and a happy quiet rests on everybody and everything. Surely earth is nearer heaven on a Sabbath than at any other time.

Then as the day closes and the deepening shades of night fall softly around us, in the tranquility of that hour we seem to hear the rustle of angels' wings, and catch a faint echo of celestial music. Thus passes away a Sabbath well spent, leaving a holy joy in the soul and a sweet peace in the heart.

LINES ON THE DEATH OF A FRIEND.

We have mingled our tears o'er the silent dead,
We have laid her to rest in her narrow bed;
And we mourn that our friend in the morn of her day,
Has been called from our midst in the tomb to lay.

Yes, Amanda, though young, has been summoned to go,
And leave those who fondly she loved here below;
Through the valley and shadow of death she hath trod,
And entered the portal of angels' abode.

Ah, well we remember the days that are gone,
When her voice in sweet harmony joined with our own,
In the songs that we sang when our hearts were as free
As the soft sighing zephyr that floats o'er the sea.

That voice is now silent, that young heart is still,
The place that is vacant no other can fill;
Oh, we miss the dear one that has passed to the tomb,
But we trust she has found a more glorious home.

Farewell, dear Amanda, we bid thee adieu,
Fond memory will weave a sweet garland for you;
Thy trials and sorrows on earth are all o'er,
Farewell till we meet on the heavenly shore.

MY ISLAND HOME.

The following lines were composed for a lady who spent the early part of her life at a lighthouse in the Bay of Fundy.

I remember the home of my childhood,
    The cot by the blue ocean side;
Where the breeze from the far distant meadows
    Swept by with the murmuring tide;
Where the dash of the spray woke the morning,
    And danced in the sun's golden light,
As he rose in his majestic splendor,
    And chased back the shadows of night.

I remember how oft with my sister,
    I've roamed on the rude rocky shore,
And gathered bright shells of the ocean,
    Or listened to dark billows roar,
Oft we've gazed on the wide spreading waters,
    When twilight had faded away,
When the moon shed her beams on the billows,
    And silvered the high dashing spray.

I remember the bed of sweet flowers,
    That bloomed on our lone little isle,
That ladened the air with their fragrance,
    And welcomed the sunbeam's bright smile,
And the sweet little bird, our canary,
    Without him the days would have long,
In his own pretty cage in the window,
    He cheered our lone cot with his song.

I remember those scenes of my girlhood,
    In fancy I see my old home,
The lone little isle and the cottage,
    Encircled by dashing white foam.
But dearer than all I remember
    The friends that I parted with there,
Though far from those loved ones I've wandered,
    One haven of rest we shall share.

Oh blest be the bonds of affection,
    A chain of pure gold is the love
Which binds kindred spirits together,
    Though severed our bodies may rove.
Though parted on earth we remember,
    Above in our heavenly home,
We will soon be there re-united,
    No more from each other to roam.

THE DYING CHILD.

On hearing of a little girl thirteen years of age, who, when about
to die, sought to comfort her weeping mother by assuring her that
all was well.

I am going home to heaven,
    Mother, wipe away thy tears,
For the pearly gates are opened,
    And an angel band appears;
I am going to join their number,
    In a land of love and light,
Soon within the golden city
    I shall walk in spotless white.

Grieve not for me, dearest mother,
    Smile upon me ere I go,
See the path to heaven shining
    Brighter than the sun below;
See the angel band approaching,
    Hear the rustle of their wings,
Nearer, nearer, they are coming,
    Peace and joy their presence brings.

When the stars are shining, mother,
    Brightly in the azure sky,
Think your darling is an angel
    Fairer than the stars on high;
Hark, I hear a soft low whisper,
    Calling me to come away
From a world of sin and sorrow,
    To the realms of endless day.

When you sink to slumber, mother,
    I will come and softly sing,
To thy heart now torn and bleeding,
    I will peace and comfort bring.
When on wings of faith your spirit
    Mounts to join the good and blest,
I will meet thee at the portal,
    Kiss me now, then let me rest.

EVENING CHARMS.

I love to wander in the shady grove,
  Just as the last bright ray is fading in the west;
When all is beautiful around me and above,
  And weary nature gently sinks to rest.
Then sweetly from the distant wood-crown'd hill,
  The wild bird's evening song falls on my listening ear,
And mingled with the murmur of the gushing rill,
  With soft low music fills the balmy air.

I love to listen to the evening breeze,
  That steals along so softly thro' the woody dell;
And sighs and whispers as it floats among the trees,
  And hushes nature with its soothing spell.
The rose that but a few short hours before
  Had waved so graceful in the gentle summer gale,
Then drops its velvet leaves, its transient life is o'er,
  And with its parting breath perfumes the vale.

THE END.